PUFFIN BOOKS
THE RAMAYANA

Bulbul Sharma is an artist and writer. She also works as an art teacher for children with special needs. She has written a novel, *Bananaflower Dreams*, three collections of short stories, and *Tales of Fabled Beasts, Gods and Demons* for children.

THE
RAMAYANA

Bulbul Sharma

PUFFIN BOOKS

PUFFIN BOOKS

USA | Canada | UK | Ireland | Australia
New Zealand | India | South Africa | China

Puffin Books is part of the Penguin Random House group of companies
whose addresses can be found at global.penguinrandomhouse.com

Published by Penguin Random House India Pvt. Ltd
7th Floor, Infinity Tower C, DLF Cyber City,
Gurgaon 122 002, Haryana, India

Penguin
Random House
India

First published in Puffin by Penguin Books India 2003
This paperback edition published in Puffin by Penguin Books India 2007

ISBN 9780143330318

Typeset in Goudy Old Style by S. R. Enterprises, New Delhi

Printed at Repro Knowledgecast Limited, India

www.penguin.co.in

Contents

The Birth of Rama 1
Tataka 3
Mareecha and Subhahu 8
Sita 10
Ahalya 11
The Swayamvar 12
Dashrath's Plan 15
The Plot 16
The Curse 21
The Banishment 22
In the Forest 28
Dashrath's Death 31
Into the Wild 40
Panchavati 43
Soorpanakha 48
Khara's Revenge 49
In Ravana's Court 53
Mareecha 56
The Golden Deer 58
The Abduction 62
The Search for Sita 66
Kabandha 70
The Monkey Clans 72
Kishkinda 80
The Search Begins 81
Hanuman in Lanka 87
Preparing for War 95
Crossing the Ocean 99
Before the Battle 101
The First Battle 103
Kumbhakaran 107

Indrajit   110
Ravana   113
Return to Ayodhya   116
The Second Banishment   121
At Valmiki's Ashram   125
The Aswamedha Horse   127
Back at the Ashram   129
Rama and His Sons   132

Afterword   136

The Birth of Rama

The city of Ayodhya, the capital of the kingdom of Kosala, was a wonderful place where people lived and worked contentedly. Everyone was peace-loving, good to their neighbours, and kind to animals. King Dashrath was a just and responsible ruler, and looked after his people as if they were his own children.

However, the king and his three queens were not happy. Their vast palace, with its glittering golden roof, silver doors and huge gardens, seemed a quiet and lonely place sometimes. King Dashrath did not have any children and this made him very sad. So after consultation with his ministers, he decided to hold a huge yagna to please the gods in the hope that they would bless him with a child.

Once the date of the yagna was decided, the city of Ayodhya began to bustle with activity. New roads were laid and hundreds of new buildings were constructed to house the many holy men, princes and ordinary people from other parts of the kingdom who were expected to attend this great yagna. Rasyasringa, a very learned sage, was invited to conduct the ceremony. The assistant priests began to collect the things needed for the yagna and read up the prayers, and the cooks in the royal kitchen began planning their menus for each day.

Finally, the great day arrived. As the people of Ayodhya watched, the grand chariots of the princes began to roll into the city one by one, followed by hundreds of sages and holy men, who came on foot. Children scampered on to the rooftops to watch the line of people walking in from faraway cities and villages.

The yagna fire was lit and barrels of ghee were poured into it. Holy men began to chant the prayers that would continue day and night. Carts full of flowers were brought and their contents distributed among those participating in the prayers. The smoke from the sacred fire, fragrant with sandalwood and incense, rose into the sky and the gods looked down approvingly from heaven.

As it happened, the gods had all gathered together that day for an important discussion. A demon-king named Ravana was creating havoc all over the three worlds, and the worried gods wanted Brahma, the creator of the universe, to do something about him.

'Many years ago, you gave Ravana a boon as a reward for the penances he had performed. This boon has made him so powerful that he is now slaughtering and plundering his way through the world. Soon he plans to overthrow us and take over heaven, too. You must stop him before it is too late,' said the gods to Brahma.

Brahma thought for a while. When he had granted the boon to Ravana, who had pleased him with his thousand-year penance, he had no idea of the trouble this would cause. The demon-king had begged him, 'Make me invincible, O great Brahma, so that no god or demon can defeat me.' Brahma had granted him his wish. Now, protected by this wonderful boon, Ravana had grown wicked and cruel, and was killing all the innocent gods and demons who stood in his way.

'Yes, I must do something to stop him,' thought the lord of creation as he looked down to see the flames from King Dashrath's yagna fire grow higher and higher. As he watched, an idea struck him. 'I will ask Vishnu, the preserver of the universe, to be born on earth as a man,' he decided. 'Ravana had asked me to make him more powerful than gods and demons. He was too proud to ask for protection against man. Vishnu can be born in King Dashrath's house as his son. He is a noble king. I would like to bless him with a son who is a part of Vishnu and who will defeat Ravana.'

Vishnu, when asked, agreed to be born on earth as King Dashrath's son in order to defeat Ravana. As soon as the gods had made this plan, the yagna fire began to glow with a golden light.

All the princes and sages who had gathered around the yagna were amazed when a tall golden figure appeared in the flames. His skin was tinged with red, and his hair glowed like a lion's mane. He held a golden bowl in his hands, which was filled with kheer. 'The gods are pleased with your prayers and have sent this gift to you,' said the golden being to King Dashrath in a sweet voice that rang through the air.

'Give this sacred kheer to your wives and you will be blessed with children.' As soon as King Dashrath took the bowl of kheer from the heavenly creature, he vanished into the flames.

King Dashrath quickly went to Queen Kaushalya's chamber and gave her half of the bowl of kheer. Then he gave one half of what remained to Sumitra, his second queen. Kaikeyi, the third queen, got half of what was left. Dashrath gave the remainder of the kheer to Sumitra.

After a while, four sons were born in the palace. The eldest was Rama, Queen Kaushalya's son. The second was Bharata, Queen Kaikeyi's son. Queen Sumitra, who had eaten the kheer twice, had twins who were named Lakshmana and Shatrughna.

Tataka

The four princes grew up fast, playing in the palace gardens, training in archery, reading the sacred texts and all the other books which princes had to read to learn to become good rulers. All the boys were loved by everyone in the palace for they were good-natured and loving. But the favourite, perhaps, was Rama. Dashrath especially adored his eldest son. Lakshmana, too, was very devoted to Rama and always tried to be by his side.

All too soon the years of their growing up were over, and the little boys who caused so much laughter around the palace became tall, majestic princes. Each of them was a gifted courtier, learned in both the ancient texts and martial skills. All the people of Ayodhya were proud of their valour and courage.

One day, a great sage named Vishwamitra came to visit King Dashrath. Everyone in the palace—queens and princes, ministers and maids, guards and gardeners, cooks and assistant cooks, stable boys and washermen, elephant-keepers and bell-ringers, priests and teachers—rushed about making the great sage comfortable. Someone fetched cool water, someone else washed his feet, while others fanned him with a silken fan in case a fly whizzed too close. They were all very nervous because Vishwamitra, though famed for his wisdom and learning, had a very bad temper.

King Dashrath hovered around anxiously, urging the sage to eat a little fruit or drink some more milk. The king was pleased that the great sage had come to visit him, but he hoped he would go away without losing his temper about anything.

At length, after he had eaten and rested, Vishwamitra explained the reason for his visit. The sage wanted to take Rama and Lakshmana with him to the forest where he lived. 'There are some demons there who keep disturbing us when we are praying or when there is a yagna. Your brave sons will get rid of these demons for us and make our lives easier,' said Vishwamitra.

King Dashrath did not know what to say. He did not want to send his young sons on such a dangerous task. He knew that they were brave and full of courage, but were they not too young to be sent into battle? Yet how was he to refuse the sage? His temper was like a bundle of dry twigs which could flare up any minute and destroy everything in sight.

As the king paced up and down, wondering what to do, Vishwamitra began to narrow his eyes and frown. But before the great sage could utter any angry words, Sage Vashishtha, who was King Dashrath's guru and skilled in dealing with people, stepped forward. He said softly, 'O king, let Rama and Lakshmana go with Vishwamitra. The entire world knows that he is the bravest of the brave and wisest of the wise. He is the master of every weapon on earth as well as in heaven. Do you think he cannot defeat the demons himself? Of course he can, without lifting a finger. Yet he asks for your sons. He asks for them because he wants to do them good. Send the princes into the forest with the sage, O king, and fear not for their safety. Instead, you should be happy that the great sage Vishwamitra has come himself to ask for them.'

At dawn the next day Rama and Lakshmana set out with Sage Vishwamitra. Though they were sad to leave their parents and brothers, they were very excited about going into the forest to fight the demons. They walked fast, their swords gleaming at their waists, bows in their hands and quivers of arrows bouncing on their backs.

Soon they reached the river Sarayu, where Vishwamitra told them to rest for a while. A gentle breeze made the leaves on the old peepal trees flutter, and the river gurgled happily as if to welcome the princes.

'Fill your palms with water from the river. I will teach you a mantra which will take away your hunger and thirst. You will never feel tired and will be able to walk long distances easily. When you meet the demons in battle you will be full of energy,' said Sage Vishwamitra. He began chanting a magic mantra as Rama and Lakshmana listened closely with their heads bowed and eyes shut in concentration. To their amazement, they soon felt filled with a new strength and all their hunger disappeared.

They walked on for several more hours. Finally, as evening fell, they stopped for the night. The princes made beds with grass and leaves for Vishwamitra and for themselves. Though they had always slept on soft, silken mattresses and sliver beds, the princes fell asleep at once.

Early next morning they set off once more, walking swiftly along the sandy banks. Their footprints made a straight line along the river. A boat was waiting for them where the river Sarayu joined the sacred river Ganga, and they got in, taking care to place their swords on their knees.

'Salute the river Ganga,' said Vishwamitra, taking a plamful of water. 'She is a goddess and once she flowed only in heaven. King Bhagiratha did penance for many years to persuade

Brahma to let Ganga come to earth, for only then would his sixty thousand kinsmen come back to life. The force of her coming to earth would have been catastrophic, so Bhagiratha begged Shiva to catch her in his matted hair. But Ganga was annoyed at being made to leave heaven, and she resolved to submerge the earth with the force of her waters. When she tried to do that, however, Shiva just held her in his tangled locks. For an entire year she twisted and turned, but she could not free herself. Then finally she became quiet and Shiva let her flow out. Now she is a gentle river, sacred and pure. Ganga's waters purify all those who touch her.'

After they crossed over the river, the banks suddenly became narrow. A dense forest stood before them. The princes were not afraid of forests. They liked all the wonderful trees and plants that grew in them, and loved to hear the birds sing and the animals call. But this forest was different. At first, it was strangely quiet. Then, as they walked deeper into the gloom, eerie sounds began to follow them. Insects cried out as if in pain and invisible birds screeched in fear. The trees grew close together, and their leaves were grey and black. Creepers with faded flowers hung from the branches like giant snakes.

'This is the forest of Dandaka,' said Vishwamitra. 'Once upon a time, it was a beautiful place where people, birds and animals lived together happily. Then, one day, a terrible demoness called Tataka came to live here, and this place became as evil as she is. When any sage performs a yagna in any of the ashrams in this forest, she comes and kills those who are praying and throws dead animals into the sacred fire.' Vishwamitra paused and pointed in the direction of a small hill close by. 'Look, there is her cave. She can smell humans from far away. Beware of her! She has the strength of a thousand elephants. You have to draw her out of her cave. Do not hesitate to kill her because she is a woman. She is evil and only you can kill her.'

Rama and Lakshmana went towards the cave. Rama put his hand on his bow and at once the entire forest began to echo with the twanging of its string.

Tataka was napping in her cave. She opened her eyes in surprise. 'What was that?' She listened and the sound seemed familiar. 'A bow! Who dares to enter my forest? Surely no human will come so deep into my lair,' she said and leapt up.

Tataka was a terrifying sight as she charged out of the cave. She was as tall as a hillock, and her fat arms were as thick as tree trunks. As she walked, the trees began to shake as if there was an earthquake. Leaves rained down and a dust storm was churned up into the sky.

Rama and Lakshmana saw her coming closer and closer, but they stood still. Tataka's nostrils were breathing fire and smoke as she howled with anger. 'Who are you, puny humans? How dare you enter my forest where no man has walked for a hundred years!' she roared. 'I will eat you up at once, and throw your bones to my beasts.'

Like all demons, Tataka knew how to use magic when she was fighting. She paused at some distance from them and caused a rain of pebbles and stones to fall on them. Rama and Lakshmana did not move as the stones rattled down. Angered by this, Tataka screamed. The ear-splitting sound echoed around the forest and made the sky crack with lightning. She rushed towards them furiously, the ground reverberating with each heavy footstep. Finally, just as she was about to crash into them, Rama shot a single arrow. It went straight into her heart, and Tataka fell down with a scream.

As soon as she died, the entire forest, which had been gloomy and sinister for many decades, was suddenly bathed in light. Trees began to flower, and fruits magically appeared on mango and palm trees. Birds emerged from their hiding places and began to sing in cheerful notes.

'Rama, you have cleared the forest by killing Tataka!' rejoiced Vishwamitra. 'Bless you, my son! You are truly born to rid the world of evil.' He could see the future, and he knew that one day Rama would have to fight a great battle to vanquish evil. Thus he was very pleased that the young prince had done so well in his first fight.

Vishwamitra continued, 'I know many mantras with which I can summon divine weapons. These weapons can vanquish any enemy. I will teach you and Lakshmana these mantras. Learn them carefully because you will need them later for the battles you have to fight.'

Rama first bowed to thank the sage. Then he and Lakshmana sat down with their hands folded, facing the east. The sage taught them all the rare mantras for divine weapons which he had learnt from Lord Shiva after years of patient worship and many sacrifices. The mantras could be used to call upon special powers during battle, when the warriors needed them the most. Every god and demon wanted to learn these mantras, but Shiva only taught them to a few very great men who had performed thousands of years of prayer and penance.

With their eyes shut and their breaths still with concentration, Rama and Lakshmana listened intently to the sage's words. He taught them how to summon each weapon, how to send it in the right direction and how to bring it back.

The two brothers memorized each detail with utmost care for they knew this was the greatest gift any warrior could ever hope to receive. With these weapons at their command, they could defeat any evil that came their way.

Mareecha and Subhahu

After walking a few more hours through the forest, which grew increasingly dense, Vishwamitra and the princes came to a small clearing in which there stood a few huts. The princes knew at once that this must be a special place.

'This is the ashram where we live and pray, meditate and study,' said Vishwamitra. 'Many great sages have lived here in the past. But now our peaceful prayers and yagnas are shattered by two demons named Mareecha and Subhahu. They fly down from the sky and throw blood and flesh into our sacred fire.'

Rama and Lakshmana grew angry as they heard this. As they stood at the ashram gates, Rama said, 'We promise you that from this day you will be able to pray in peace. We vow that we will clear this beautiful and holy place of all evil.'

Vishwamitra and the other rishis in the ashram were very pleased to hear these words. 'We are certain you will rid us of these demons,' they said, and began preparing for the yagna.

After they had bathed and eaten, Rama told Vishwamitra, 'Please begin your yagna. We will guard you and keep the sacred fire safe.'

For the next seven days and nights, Rama and Lakshmana kept vigil. They carried their bows and arrows with them all the time. They took it in turns to rest, so that the yagna was never unprotected. But no demons appeared.

On the eighth day, Lakshmana began to get impatient. 'Where are these demons?' he asked Rama. 'My hands are itching to use my bow.'

Rama laughed. 'Waiting is the most difficult part, because it is hard to stay attentive all the time. But we must be calm and never take our eyes off the horizon.'

As he said these words, the yagna fire suddenly began to sputter. Flames rose up in the sky. Agni, the god of fire, was sending them a warning.

Rama looked up, and there, like two massive hills of stone, stood Mareecha and Subhahu. Their hair streamed out, knotted and as red as blood. Their eyes glowed like coals and the claws on their hands were filled with rotting flesh. Screaming with terror, most of the sages ran into the ashram. Only Vishwamitra waited by the yagna to see what the princes would do.

Rama and Lakshmana looked up straight at Mareecha as he charged towards them, screaming foul words. The princes stood unmoved, but their minds worked rapidly. He was so huge and ferocious that it would take hundreds of ordinary arrows to harm him. So Rama began chanting one of the mantras for divine weapons that Vishwamitra had taught him. Thunder roared and lightning flashed as the Manavastra went flying towards Mareecha.

Mareecha did not see or hear anything coming towards him, but suddenly he felt as if he had been struck by lightning. Before he could do anything to save himself, the Manavastra had carried him a hundred thousand yojanas, and hurled him into the sea. He sank instantly like a stone from the force of the weapon, all the way down to the caves at the bottom of the sea. He was amazed to find he was still alive.

Subhahu began to look scared, but he decided to attack the yagna all the same. But just as he moved towards it, Rama hurled another divine weapon at him. The Agneyastra, a weapon created by the god of fire, began to burn the demon from inside as well as from outside as soon as it touched him. Within moments, he was just a heap of ashes on the ground.

The rishis came out from the ashram, clapping their hands in joy. They blessed Rama and Lakshmana, and thanked them for bringing peace once more to their ashram.

Once the yagna finished peacefully, the rishis began preparing for a journey to the kingdom of Videha. They asked Vishwamitra and the princes to accompany them to its marvellous capital city of Mithila where its great ruler, King Janaka, was conducting a special yagna. Shiva's mighty bow, which no man had ever been able to string, would be on display.

Vishwamitra agreed promptly, smiling to himself. Rama and Lakshmana, too, were thrilled to go to Mithila to see this rare bow.

Sita

Mithila was a beautiful city, glittering with palaces and temples covered in gold and diamonds. But more beautiful than its bejewelled palaces was the princess of Mithila, Sita.

She was as delicate as a flower, with skin the colour of gold. Her hair was long and black and thick, like a silken cloud. When she smiled, it was as if the moon had appeared from behind the clouds. She was also gentle and soft-spoken.

Sita was a gift to Janaka from the goddess of the earth. King Janaka had been told in a dream that he would find a sacred site in a field. When he was ploughing the fields to find this site, he came upon a hollow in the ground. In that hollow lay a beautiful baby girl, sheltered by leaves and flowers.

King Janaka picked her up gently and, thanking the goddess of the earth for giving him this wonderful gift, took the baby home to his wife. They were childless, and there was much rejoicing when this baby came into their lives.

Sita grew up to be as kind as she was beautiful. She had now reached the age when her father had begun to search for a suitable husband for her. But it was not going to be an easy task to win the hand of the princess of Mithila.

The king wanted to find the most heroic man in the world for his precious daughter. He devised a hard test to select the best son-in-law. He possessed Shiva's bow, which was so heavy that it needed a hundred men to pull it. 'I will give my daughter's hand in marriage to the man who can string this mighty bow,' King Janaka had announced. The great yagna to which Rama and Lakshmana were going would be followed by Sita's suitors trying to string Shiva's bow.

Soon the road to Mithila was crowded with chariots and horses as all the neighbouring kings and princes rushed to Mithila in the hope of winning Sita's hand.

Ahalya

As Rama and Lakshmana were walking with Vishwamitra along the forest paths which only the rishis knew, they saw an ashram surrounded by tall trees full of fruit. Berries and flowers grew profusely on the shrubs around the simple hut. But the place was strangely silent, and there were no birds or deer to be seen.

'Why is this ashram so desolate and empty? Does no one live here?' asked Rama.

Vishwamitra explained, 'Once upon a time, a sage named Gautama lived here with his beautiful wife Ahalya. One day, when he was away, Indra, the king of gods, disguised himself as Gautama and came to the ashram. Ahalya, though she knew it was not her husband, felt flattered by Indra's attentions since he was the king of the gods. She fell in love with him. Sage Gautama read her mind and, enraged by her lack of faithfulness, cursed her. "You shall turn to stone. This beauty which has made you so vain and wayward will be nothing but a cold piece of rock," he said. Ahalya became a statue of stone the moment he said these words. See, there she waits beneath the tree.' Vishwamitra pointed to a beautiful stone figure of a woman.

Rama stepped forward in wonder and reached out to touch the statue. There was a sudden rustling sound and the stone figure began to move. Slowly Ahalya's face emerged out of the stone.

As Vishwamitra, Rama and Lakshmana watched in wonder, the statue came to life. She opened her beautiful eyes, which were full of tears, and bowed her head to them. 'You have set me free of the curse which turned me into stone,' she said.

The ashram suddenly began to hum with life. All the insects and birds, which had been silent all these years, began to chirp. Deer and peacocks began to play in the clearing in front of the hut.

Sage Gautama appeared out of nowhere and blessed Rama. Now that Ahalya had been freed of the curse, they could live happily in their ashram.

The Swayamvar

Vishwamitra and the princes continued their journey to Mithila. When they reached, they saw that the city was bustling with people. Chariots rolled in, each more resplendent than the previous one. Some were drawn by four horses; others by prettily decorated teams of eight horses.

The yagna was magnificent. People had travelled there from all the neighbouring countries, and many holy men who had not left their ashrams in the mountains for years had come for it. But for many of the princes and warriors who were there, their real interest was in the swayamvar which would follow the yagna.

After the yagna, handsome kings covered in pearls and diamonds, young princes wearing robes of silk, and noblemen from all the neighbouring kingdoms began trooping towards the palace to try to win Sita's hand. Each one thought he was the strongest and was going to be the chosen one. Each of them had polished and twirled his moustache. Every prince tightened his bejewelled sword-belt around his waist as he walked into the glittering hall of King Janaka's palace.

As they settled into their seats in the hall, each contender eyed the others from the corner of his eyes. Though everyone felt a little nervous, they puffed up their chests and rattled their gold shields to give themselves courage.

Rama and Lakshmana walked in quietly with Vishwamitra and sat down in one corner. Everyone was curious about the two young men who had accompanied the great sage. 'Who are they?' 'Why has the great sage brought these boys with him?' 'Surely these lads do not hope to compete with us?' they muttered to one another.

There was a great rumbling sound as Shiva's bow was wheeled in. It took a hundred of the palace heavyweights to drag the cart into the hall.

The trumpets rang out as King Janaka appeared. There was silence in the crowded hall as he spoke. 'This is Shiva's bow, which was gifted to my ancestors. No one has been able to lift it, leave along string it. The hero who can string this mighty bow shall wed my daughter Sita,' he announced. A murmur ran through the hall.

One by one, all the princes and noblemen and kings came up and tried to pick up the bow. They flexed their muscles, tightened their belts and muttered prayers before they started, but not a single one of them could even move it. Some even collapsed from the effort and had to be carried out.

Finally, Vishwamitra nodded to Rama. The young prince got up and went towards the bow. He walked with such quiet dignity, holding his head high, that Sita, who was watching from a window, gave her heart to the handsome prince. 'He is as handsome as a young god. He walks like a lion, yet his eyes are so gentle,' she said to herself. 'O mighty bow of Shiva, make yourself light so that this young man can string you.'

But Sita did not have to worry. Rama picked up the bow as if it were a feather and strung it swiftly. His movements were so quick that it all passed in a blur. The next moment, all the kings, princes, noblemen and sages heard a great clap of thunder that fell on the palace dome as the bow broke into two pieces.

The earth shook as if mountains had collapsed. The seas rose, and the fleet of horses that pulls the sun's chariot began to leave its daily path across the sky. Many in the hall swooned from fear. Everyone was speechless with wonder as they realized that not only had Rama picked up and strung the heavy bow, but that his might was so great that he had broken it into two like a twig. The gods watching from heaven began to applaud, and the gandharvas, who are heavenly singers, began to sing Rama's praises.

King Janaka, pleased that the prince of Ayodhya had won his daughter's hand, announced their wedding. Sita tried to calm her fluttering heart which leapt with joy when Rama smiled tenderly at her from far away.

Messengers were sent to Dashrath to announce the good news. He came at once, accompanied by his queens, to attend the wedding.

The wedding was celebrated with great pomp and ceremony, and kings and princes, holy men and poor people travelled from far and near to bless the young couple. Glorious flowers rained down from the skies, heavenly music played, gandharvas sang and apsaras danced. For ten days Mithila resembled Indra's celestial city.

Dashrath's Plan

Rama and Sita came back to Ayodhya and began to live in the palace. Days passed happily.

King Dashrath, too, was happy but he often thought that what would bring him the greatest joy was to see Rama become the crown prince or yuvraj. 'Once he is installed as the yuvraj and learns how to rule, I can give up the throne and spend the rest of my life in prayer. I know in my heart that he will rule this kingdom even better than I have. He is brave and courageous, wise beyond his years,' thought King Dashrath.

The king called his ministers to ask their advice. Everyone agreed at once that Rama would make a good yuvraj. 'He is noble and full of courage, dutiful to his elders and kind to those younger than him. He is learned in the religious texts and skilled in warfare. He has no faults and he is loved by all the people of Ayodhya,' declared the council of ministers and noblemen, and they agreed that the coronation should take place soon.

Everyone in the palace was overjoyed at the news. Queen Kaushalya was very happy that her son was going to be the yuvraj. When he came to her chambers to seek her blessings, she touched his bowed head tenderly and said, 'May you live long, my son. Be a kind and just ruler. Conquer your foes with courage and protect your people from evil.' The other two queens were equally happy. Bharata was away, visiting his grandfather, Kaikeyi's father, but Lakshmana and Shatrughna were also delighted.

As the news spread all over the city, people began to sing and dance on the streets. Children enacted mock coronations with their friends, while their mothers decorated their homes with marigold flowers, lamps and mango leaves.

Over the next few days, the palace halls were decorated with new jewels, the singers and dancers practised in their quarters, and gardeners tended the plants with extra care to make them bloom faster. The palace cooks prepared mountains of sweets: some were white with crystals of sugar, others as pink as rose petals and studded with almonds. Children begged their parents to take them to the palace gates so that they could see the preparations. If they were lucky they might catch a glimpse of Rama as he walked in the gardens where sliver fountains played and peacocks danced.

People from all the neighbouring cities and villages began to pour in and new houses were built to accommodate them. Kings, princes, jugglers, magicians, hawkers selling sweets and fruit, beggars, rich men and women, sages and holy men from all over came into the city to see the coronation.

The Plot

While everyone in Ayodhya was busy preparing for Rama's coronation, an old woman watched quietly from a palace window. She was Manthara—a hunchback who was Queen Kaikeyi's maid. No one in the palace liked her very much, so no one had told her what was happening. The only person who talked to her was Kaikeyi, and she had been too busy to spare Manthara any time.

Finally, Manthara could bear the suspense no longer. She hobbled out of the room and went to the main hall. 'What is all this noise and fuss about?' she asked one of the boys who was climbing a pillar to hang a garland of flowers.

'Rama is to be crowned yuvraj tomorrow. Don't you know anything?' said the boy cheekily, knowing he was safe on top of the pillar.

Manthara was stunned to hear this news. She scowled at the boy and rushed to Queen Kaikeyi's chambers. The queen was feeding her pet parakeet a piece of mango and looked up happily as Manthara came charging into the room. 'Yes, I know the good news,' she said, when Manthara asked her. 'My Rama is to be made the yuvraj tomorrow. You must dress me in my finest jewels, dear Manthara, and here—take this pearl necklace. I am so happy today.' The queen threw Manthara a string of pearls that she was wearing around her neck.

The old woman did not even look at the gift. She raised her head high and began wailing, 'O queen, you are as foolish as a dove! I have raised you from the time you were a baby in your father's palace and have never felt angry with you. But today I feel rage that is like a fire within me.' Her eyes snapped and crossed with anger.

'But what is wrong, Manthara? Don't you like the necklace? I will give you a golden one tomorrow when Rama becomes the yuvraj of Ayodhya,' said Kaikeyi nervously. Manthara had been her nurse and had always dominated the gentle queen. Though Kaikeyi had been a queen for many years, she still obeyed Manthara without question.

'O, that you are so blind, so foolish! Can't you see the danger that lies ahead for you when Rama becomes the yuvraj? Can't you see how Kaushalya is going to behave? She will make you her slave and your son Bharata will become a servant to Rama in this palace!' hissed Manthara.

Queen Kaikeyi was shocked to hear Manthara speak like this. 'Hush, Manthara! Do not utter these harsh words when you speak of Rama! He is as dear to me as my Bharata. I am overjoyed that the king has chosen him to be the yuvraj. So speak no more or I will have to banish you from my palace,' said Kaikeyi, who knew that she would never have the courage to do that.

'Send me away, if you wish,' said Manthara, her face dark with anger. 'But listen to my words of warning before it is too late, before you become a slave to Kaushalya and your son has to bow before Rama. Ask the king why he is doing it in such haste. Why is he crowning Rama when Bharata is away in your father's kingdom? Ask the king who his favourite queen is. Ask him which queen saved his life when he was wounded—was it you or was it Kaushalya, whose son he is gifting the kingdom of Ayodhya to?'

Kaikeyi sat quietly for a while, as Manthara hobbled around her, muttering in rage. Worry crept into her beautiful eyes. Manthara could see that her words were slowly seeping into the queen's mind and continued. 'Even if you do not care about yourself, what kind of a mother are you? Don't you know that Rama could kill your son so that there is no rival to the throne? Lakshmana and Shatrughna could never be king, so Rama will not harm them. Why is Dashrath so anxious to crown Rama before Bharata comes back? Don't you think someone gave him the idea?'

'Will Rama ever harm my Bharata?' Kaikeyi wondered. 'No, no, he is so kind and gentle. But what if he changes once he becomes the ruler? Why does the king not wait till Bharata is back? What shall I do?' whispered the queen to herself.

This was the moment Manthara had been waiting for. She seized her chance and took the queen's hands into her own. She looked deep into Kaikeyi's eyes and said in a whisper, 'Ask the king to make Bharata the yuvraj. Ask him to banish Rama to the forest for fourteen years. Do this—do this for your own sake, and for your only son. Do it now, before it is too late and all is lost—son, kingdom, your life.'

Manthara repeated her words over and over again until Kaikeyi was trembling with fear. Finally, the queen nodded obediently and lay sobbing on her bed. 'What shall I do, Manthara? I'm afraid.'

Manthara stroked her head and spoke softly, 'Remember when long ago King Dashrath was wounded in battle and fell unconscious? You drove his chariot out of the battlefield.

It was you who took the arrows out of his body and saved his life. When he revived, he had granted you two wishes—do you remember, my sweet queen? And you had said, "I need nothing now. I will ask later." The time has come now to ask for those two wishes. Tell him your first wish is that he should give the throne to your son, and the second one is that he should banish Rama.' Manthara's eyes gleamed with malice and triumph as she spoke, but Kaikeyi was too upset to notice.

Dashrath was busy discussing the coronation with his ministers when he received a message from Queen Kaikeyi, asking him to come to her immediately. He was surprised, for she never disturbed him when he was holding court. 'It must be something very urgent. I hope she is not unwell,' said Dashrath to himself as he hurried to her chambers.

He was surprised to find her lying on the floor in a dark room, dressed in an old sari, her hair untied and dishevelled as if she were in mourning. Amazed and distressed, Dashrath knelt beside her. 'What has happened to you, my queen? Are you ill? I will send for the best doctor in my kingdom. What is it? Speak, for my heart breaks to see you like this.'

Kaikeyi did not reply. She lay on the floor with her beautiful face turned to the wall, her long hair covering her like a blanket.

'Has someone hurt you? Do you want something? Tell me, please! Do not remain silent like this. You know I will do anything for you.'

As soon as King Dashrath said this, the queen opened her eyes and sat up. 'O king, give me your word that you will give me what I ask for,' she said softly.

The king, pleased that Kaikeyi was not ill and dying, agreed without thinking. 'I will give you what you want. I swear on my beloved son Rama that I will grant you your wish,' he said, not realizing that grief was waiting for him like a coiled serpent.

Kaikeyi looked at him long and hard. 'Then give me the two wishes you had promised me long ago when I saved your life on the battlefield,' she said quickly, before she lost her courage. 'The first thing I ask is that you make my son, Bharata, the yuvraj. The second thing I ask is that you banish Rama to the forest for fourteen years.'

Dashrath recoiled as if struck by lightning. His face turned ashen and he could not breathe. 'This is a nightmare. Or am I losing my mind?' he thought, and he fell down unconscious.

When he revived after a few minutes, Kaikeyi was bathing his face with cool scented water. 'Did you speak those cruel words or was I dreaming? You could never hurt me thus, gentle queen,' whispered the king.

Kaikeyi turned her face away. 'I did indeed speak them. If you wish to go back on your word, you may do so. But then you will never again be known as the man who always keeps his word, no matter what the price. And if you do not grant me my wishes, or if Rama does not agree, I will kill myself.' Her voice was icy.

King Dashrath had never heard her speak in such a tone before. The beautiful face which he loved so much looked hard and cruel. He felt a sharp pain in his heart as if Kaikeyi had stabbed him with a dagger, but following that came rage. 'O you wicked, sinful woman, to ask me such a thing! Banish my Rama... What a cruel heart you have to say such thing! Kill yourself... How can I break my word? You think Rama will ever disobey me? Do you think Bharata will ever agree?'

Kaikeyi was not daunted by his words. She looked bored.

Dashrath changed his tone. 'O, pity me, my queen. Take back your words. I wish I had died before hearing these words from your mouth. Why have you changed like this? You were as gentle as a dove, and now you hiss like a serpent.' Abandoning his royal dignity and pride, he fell at the queen's feet and pleaded. 'Ask for only one wish, my queen. I will give Bharata the kingdom, but let Rama stay with me.'

For hours King Dashrath begged, scolded and cajoled Kaikeyi, but to no avail. She was unmoved. 'You promised me two wishes, and now I want them,' said the queen, tossing her head. Manthara watched from a hidden corner and smiled wickedly.

Finally, tired and broken, King Dashrath had to agree to make Bharata the yuvraj and banish Rama to the forest. As he stumbled out of the queen's chambers into the dark night, he looked many years older than the proud king who had walked in. His eyes blind with tears, he roamed about the palace all night, crying in anguish.

The Curse

Dashrath was in such pain that he thought he would not live to see dawn. Suddenly, he remembered the grief he had caused to a blind old man many years ago.

While hunting in the forest, the king had heard a sound coming from the direction of a stream. 'It must be a deer drinking water,' he had thought and sent an arrow flying towards the sound. The arrow went through the trees swiftly, like a shaft of light. Then, suddenly, there was a loud cry. Dashrath had rushed towards the stream, where he saw a horrible sight. It was not a deer he had wounded, but a young boy. 'Please, sir, help me take this water back to my blind parents,' the boy had gasped, pointing towards a grove. Then he fell back as life went out of his body.

His heart filled with sorrow at the terrible mistake he had made by taking an innocent human's life, Dashrath had picked up the boy's body and his pot of water, and carried them to the grove that he had pointed to. When he arrived there, he saw a blind couple. As they heard his footsteps, the old man, who was a learned sage, spoke, 'Have you brought water, son? Give it to us. We are thirsty.'

King Dashrath gave them some water. In a voice which was heavy with sorrow, he told them what had happened.

The old couple cried until they could cry no more. Finally, the old man said, 'You, sir, may be a great king, but you have taken away our eyes and our heart. We will die—my wife and I—because we cannot live without our son.

'He was the one who fetched us water and food. He gathered for us all that we needed for our prayers, food and medicine. When we were younger, he led us from place to place, holding our hands. When we became too old and ill to walk, he carried us around in two baskets strung on either end of a long pole. He was our life, and without him, we will surely die.

'But before I die, I curse you.' The old man's voice changed and was filled with anger. 'I curse you, O king, that you too will die grieving for a much-loved son.'

With these words, the old man and his wife lay down and died.

King Dashrath remembered the old man's words as he stumbled around the palace. 'His curse has come true,' he muttered to himself, and wondered how he would live through the coming day.

The Banishment

The next morning, everyone in Ayodhya woke up with a great sense of anticipation, for it was the day of Rama's coronation. But within a few hours, everyone at the palace was stunned to hear what the king announced to his ministers.

'Rama is not to be made the yuvraj!' 'Rama is to be banished!' 'Has the king lost his mind?' whispered the ministers, the generals, the teachers, the holy men and the guards. Soon the news spread all over the city.

The people of Ayodhya gathered at all their usual meeting spots—at wells, in parks and in the marketplaces—to talk. 'How can our king, so wise and noble, think of such a terrible thing?' they asked one another, confused and unhappy. The women wept when they thought of Sita living without her husband, and the children were told to stop playing their coronation games.

Only Manthara and Kaikeyi were happy. They watched, hidden behind a secret doorway, when the king called Rama and told him that he was not to be made the yuvraj. Moreover, he was exiled to the forest for fourteen years.

'I will obey your wishes, my father,' Rama said calmly. 'I will leave for the forest tomorrow, as you command me.' His voice was so gentle and his manner was so calm that even Kaikeyi began to feel sad. 'No, it is for your own good, for your son's good,' whispered Manthara in her ear when she saw the tears in the queen's eyes.

When Rama went to his mother's chambers to bid her goodbye, Sita was waiting for him. 'I, too, will come with you, my lord,' she said shyly.

'No, Sita, you must not!' said Rama, shocked. 'You will not be able to live the hard life of a forest-dweller. There are fierce monsters and beasts in the forest, crocodiles in the rivers, and pythons lurk on the branches of every tree. The paths are full of thorny bushes. The sun and winds will be harsh for someone who is not used to being outdoors. You are a princess, accustomed to the softest of beds and the most delicious food. In the forest, I will have to live on roots and berries, and sleep on the hard earth where serpents crawl. I cannot bear to see you suffer like that. You should stay here in the palace with my mother and father.'

Sita's gentle face flushed with determination, and when she spoke, her soft voice was so firm and strong that Rama was surprised. His shy Sita would not leave his side and insisted on going with him to the forest. 'I will wear the rough bark and deerskin you wear. I will eat whatever simple food you eat in the forest. I will sleep on a bed of leaves on the hard earth. I will walk barefoot on the ground. All I want is to be with you. With you by my side, I will be safe from every danger. The thorns on the forest path will seem as soft as flower buds, the hot winds as soothing as a paste of sandalwood. I have shared your happy life until now, and I will gladly share your misfortune. Please do not leave me behind, for I will surely die.' Sita's doe-like eyes brimmed with tears at the last words.

Though Rama did not want her to come with him, he had to agree for he had no arguments left. 'Come then, let us prepare for our journey. Give away your jewels and cast away your silken robes. We shall give all our wealth to the poor for we shall have no further use for it.'

Delighted that she was not going to be parted from him, Sita happily stripped off the precious gold ornaments she was wearing. As they prepared to go to Queen Kaushalya, Lakshmana came rushing to them.

'I have just heard,' he said. 'What has happened to our father? How could he do this?'

Rama raised a hand to stop him. 'It is our father's wish. I am going to obey him. Fourteen years will pass soon enough,' he said.

Lakshmana grasped his brother's hand. 'Then I, too, will come with you, dear brother. I will serve you, and guard you day and night. I will clear the forest paths for you. I will gather fruits and fetch water. Ever since I have been a child, I have been with you. Now how can you go without me? Please take me with you,' said Lakshmana, his voice trembling with sadness.

Once again, Rama had no arguments left.

Queen Kaushalya bore the news bravely. 'I am glad Lakshmana and Sita are going with you,' she told Rama. 'But alas, the palace will become empty for me!'

The next day they set off early in the morning. Though they had cast off their silken clothes and jewels, the rough barks and skins they wore only heightened their beauty. Sita's only adornment was a pair of thin gold bangles. Rama had bid farewell to his parents and Queen Sumitra quietly, without any tears. Now, as the old king watched his eldest son leave the palace, he felt life ebbing out of his body. 'I see death's shadow on me. I will never see my sons again,' he thought, and fell down unconscious.

The king's chariot, driven by Sumantra, his loyal attendant, was to take Rama, Sita and Lakshmana to the edge of the forest. The chariot could hardly move through the streets of Ayodhya because all the men, women and children of the city had gathered at that early hour to say goodbye to their favourite prince. Many wept, and some clung to the wheels of the chariot to prevent it from leaving. Some urged the horses, 'They say you have sharp ears. Do not, we pray you, take our princes away.' Many spoke out in anger against the king for doing such a thing. Some people ran behind the chariot, determined to follow Rama and Sita wherever they went.

Finally, Rama stopped the chariot and turned to speak to the people, for he could not bear to see old men and women running behind the chariot. 'I must obey my father's wishes,' he said. 'He has made his decision, and I must see that his word is honoured. He is your king, as he is mine, and we must all do what he says,' said Rama in a quiet voice.

Many turned back, but some still followed, saying, 'We, too, shall go with you. Let this city be empty of people; let only snakes, scorpions and rats live here. Our kingdom is where our prince is.'

The chariot and the crowd following it reached the banks of the river Sarayu. But it seemed even the river did not want Rama to leave, for its waters rose in a flood. The chariot had to stop on the banks and Sumantra let the horses loose to graze.

'We shall spend the night here,' said Rama. 'See how beautiful it is. How the trees and animals welcome us back to the forest!' They all offered evening prayers by the river. The stars made the river gleam like a line of silver. Lakshmana gathered some soft green grass and spread it on the earth for Rama and Sita. Then, bow in his hand, he sat vigil all night, watching over them and all the people who had come with them from Ayodhya as they slept under the open sky.

Rama rose when the sky was still dark. He woke Sumantra and said, 'Let us leave while the people of Ayodhya sleep. I am deeply touched by their affection, but I cannot let them follow me to the forest. Sumantra, I have to ask you to play a game of deception. Take the chariot back towards the city. The wheels will leave a track on the dew-soaked ground, and when the people wake up and see the track, they will think we have gone back to Ayodhya and go back too. Once they reach Ayodhya, they will realize that I have deceived them, but I do not want them to suffer the harsh life of the forest for fourteen years.' He paused and pointed to a tree in the distance. 'In the meanwhile, you come back for us by a different path and meet us by that tree. We shall be waiting there.'

It all went as planned. Sumantra returned by a different path after the people of Ayodhya had returned to the city. The horses quietly pulled the chariot across the water. The only sounds that could be heard were the water lapping against the bank and the early morning chirps of birds. They could see a line of tall trees, dark against the rising sun, in the forest that was going to be their home for fourteen years. The ferocious demons, friendly monkeys and eagles, learned sages and simple people who lived in the forest would now be a part of the new adventure that Rama, Lakshmana and Sita were travelling towards in their golden chariot.

After they crossed the river, Sumantra drove the chariot far into the forest. After crossing many streams, they reached the southern boundary of the kingdom, where Rama bowed his head and bid his country goodbye.

Rama asked Sumantra to take them to the banks of the river Ganga. It was cool and peaceful by the riverside and they decided to rest there in the shade of a huge tree. Their horses grazed nearby. Sita was thrilled to see a flock of geese flying across the river.

Suddenly, they heard the sound of footsteps. Turning in the direction of the sound, they saw a long line of men walking towards them, carrying baskets of fruits, soft mattresses of woven grass, pitchers of water and jars of honey. One man, who seemed to be their leader, bowed to them.

'I am Guha, the chief of the tribes of this forest,' he said. 'We know who you are and we have heard of your banishment. We are greatly honoured that you have come to our land.

Please stay here for the length of your exile. We will build you a home. You will not lack anything here.'

Rama smiled, but shook his head. 'I thank you for your kindness, but I have made a promise to my father. I have to spend fourteen years in the forest living a simple life so I cannot accept your generous offer. You can help us in two ways though. Please allow us to rest here today. Tomorrow, if you could find us a boat in which to cross the river, we would be very grateful.'

Guha was sad that they would not stay, but agreed willingly to help them. They all sat together and ate some fruit, and Rama asked Guha's tribesmen to feed the horses some fresh grass. Guha promised to find a boat for the following morning.

Early the following morning, Rama asked Sumantra to take the chariot back to Ayodhya. But Sumantra did not want to leave them. 'Please let me stay here. I cannot live in peace in Ayodhya, knowing that the three of you are in the forest,' he said.

'No, dear Sumantra, from now on we must walk. You must return and be with the king. He needs you in this hour of sadness. Please look after him and our dear mothers. Ask Bharata to be a good yuvraj and live up to the glorious traditions of our family,' said Rama. He embraced Sumantra, gently patted the horses and walked away from the last link with his princely life.

Sumantra watched them get into the boat, which Guha had brought, and cross the great river Ganga. He could see their figures getting smaller and smaller as the boat rose and fell with the waves.

As they set sail, Sita offered prayers to the river Ganga. 'O goddess, please grant that we return safely after fourteen years. I will pray to you again, great river, when we come back. Please protect my lord and Lakshmana,' she murmured. The boat swayed and the movement splashed the cool and clear water over her hands, as if the river was blessing her.

In the Forest

The forest across the river was so dense that they could not see any path leading into it. 'Lakshmana, please walk ahead and lead the way,' said Rama as they stepped out on to the rocky shore. 'Sita will walk in the middle, and I will be behind her so that she is always protected.'

For the first time they realized that they were alone. Their beloved parents, their friends, the people of Ayodhya, the palace with its jewelled halls and hundreds of servants—all seemed so far away.

They left the boat tied to the shore and started to walk along the banks. The shadows began to lengthen. Evening fell suddenly, as it does in forests. As twilight vanished, the owls began to hoot. As it was too dark to walk, Rama decided that they should rest under the huge banyan tree they could see right ahead. Sita, tired after the long journey, fell asleep at once but Rama and Lakshmana stayed awake, talking in soft voices.

'I wonder how they are at the palace. Our father must be so sad and ill. Our mothers must be crying their hearts out. I think, maybe you should return to take care of them. I can look after Sita and myself,' said Rama, sadly.

Lakshmana touched his brother's hand and said, 'I will never leave you. I will remain here with you as long as you have to stay. Ayodhya means nothing to me. You are my brother, and I shall stand by your side, come what may.' These reassuring words made Rama feel a little less sad, and they gradually drifted off to sleep.

The loud cry of the koel woke them at dawn, and they set off at once before the sun rose and it got too hot. They were not sure in what direction to walk, so they continued to keep to the banks of the river. After a while they came to a place where the sound of gushing waters made them stop.

'This must be Prayag, the sacred place where the two great rivers merge. See how the golden waters of Ganga flow along with the dark, silvery waves of Yamuna. Let us go and meet Sage Bharadwaj who lives here. He will advise us where to go next,' said Rama.

The sage lived in a little ashram near where the rivers met. He was very pleased to see them. 'You must stay here with us in Prayag. We will look after you as well as we can,' he said.

But Rama shook his head. 'I am grateful to you but we must look for a place which is further inside the forest, where people cannot find us. Please tell us where to go.'

The sage thought for a while and then said, 'I know a peaceful and secluded place where you can live. It is on top of a beautiful hill, surrounded by cool green forests full of fruits trees, waterfalls and streams. It is called Chitrakoot.' He gave them directions to get there.

They thanked the sage and then set off again, following the directions he had given them. The trees seemed to be taller here, and on their high branches hung creepers covered with pretty white flowers. Sometimes little animals darted out of the bushes to startle them, but they were not afraid. The sage had told them to stay on the path which had been trodden by the feet of sages throughout the centuries, for it was a safe route.

Soon they came to an ancient banyan tree where the sage had asked them to offer prayers. 'Look, there is the tree. How huge it is! The branches are like the pillars in our palace,' exclaimed Sita. She folded her hands and prayed, 'O great banyan, please make our journey safe. Protect us from the dangers of the forest.' The old tree fluttered its leaves, and Sita felt that her prayers had been heard.

They walked ahead along the path. The trees grew so dense that the forest seemed to be not green but dark blue. A thick grove of bamboo grew just where the path turned towards the river. Rama noticed how broad the river was. 'We will have to build a boat to go across,' he said to Lakshmana. 'Sita, you rest under that tree while Lakshmana and I collect some wood.'

The two brothers broke some stems of bamboo and tied them together with a few slender but strong vines. Lakshmana, who was very good with his hands, made the boat secure by tying rootlets around the bamboo. He spread some soft grass and a few creepers with big leaves on the boat for Sita to sit. He even made an umbrella with some leaves to protect her from the sun.

The boat was small but sturdy, and it took them across the river quickly.

As soon as they reached the other bank, the air became cool and fragrant. A clear path led into the forest from the riverbank.

'There is Chitrakoot. I can see it on top of the hill,' said Rama. They started walking towards it. Waterfalls gurgled and splashed, and the koels called out to them. They saw a herd of elephants drinking water near the streams which criss-crossed the forest path.

Sita looked around her, her eyes full of wonder. 'What pretty flowers! Look—look at that baby peacock,' she said. The palash tree showered orange flowers in their path, ripe mangoes dropped into their hands and bees hummed around their heads.

'What a gigantic beehive! See, there are so many of them!' said Rama, looking up at the branches.

'This forest is indeed beautiful. We will make it our home.'

They settled down in a clearing near the hilltop where Lakshmana built a tiny hut with branches and covered it with grass. Nearby was the ashram of Sage Valmiki, who was pleased to have them there and showed them where the best fruit trees were. 'There is plenty to eat in the forest and sweet water in the springs. You will be happy here,' he said.

The three of them were indeed very happy in Chitrakoot. Life soon settled into a routine. Lakshmana went out early each day to gather fruits, flowers and berries, which they all shared. Sita looked after them. She kept the hut clean and fed the deer that came to the door. The days went by peacefully, full of simple joys and sharing.

But in the sky dark clouds were gathering. Though they did not know it, the winds gradually began to blow these clouds towards idyllic Chitrakoot. The thunderclap of war was still distant, but events moved elsewhere that would soon bring trouble into their contented lives.

Dashrath's Death

After Rama, Lakshmana and Sita had sailed away in the boat, Sumantra had stood for a long time watching them, his eyes full of tears. Then, with a heavy heart, he turned his horses towards Ayodhya and rode back.

The city, which had always been bustling with life, now seemed very quiet, as if no one lived there. As the chariot entered the city gates, people came running up to Sumantra. 'Where is Rama? Where have you left him?' they shouted, stopping the chariot.

Finally, with great difficulty, Sumantra made his way to the palace. The great halls with their painted ceilings looked bare and forlorn. The king was sitting quietly by the window in the room where he held court. His queens, Kaushalya and Sumitra, sat silently with him. Sumantra was shocked to see how Dashrath had aged in just three days.

Dashrath raised his head slowly when Sumantra bowed before him. 'O Sumantra, dear friend, do you bring news of my son?' he said, tears beginning to stream down his face. 'How is he? Is Sita well? Lakshmana? Speak, dear Sumantra, tell me about them. Your words will be like a cool touch to my fever.' The king's voice broke as he spoke. The queens looked at him with sorrowful eyes.

Sumantra, his voice heavy with pain, began, 'Rama sends his love and respect to you, noble king, and to the three queens. He asks Bharata to take care of you and carry on your great name as king. The last I saw them was when they crossed the river Ganga in the boat which Guha, the chief of the land, had brought for them. I saw Sita offering prayers to the sacred river, and when they got to the other side I saw Lakshmana walk ahead into the forest, followed by Sita. Rama walked last. Then the three of them disappeared among the trees and I could not see them any more.' Sumantra's voice trailed away.

King Dashrath threw his head back and began to sob quietly. 'I, too, will see them no more... I feel life ebbing away from this body... These eyes will not see my sons and daughter again. This grief will kill me as it did that innocent boy's old parents. This is the curse and I see death standing at the door. O Rama, O Lakshmana, and my poor Sita!'

That night, while the entire palace slept, the old king, a noble and great ruler whom his people once loved, died crying for his banished children.

A fleet of fast horses carried messengers at once to fetch Bharata since now he was to be the new king. Bharata was staying with his grandfather, the king of Kakeya.

When Bharata had woken up that morning, he had been filled with great unhappiness. 'What is the matter, Bharata?' his friends asked. 'You seem to be lost somewhere. Shall we go into the forest to hunt or shall we take a boat out on the river?'

But Bharata was not in the mood to do anything. He had had a terrible nightmare. 'I saw my father in great distress. His face was lined with dirt and oil. He was dressed in strange black and red robes, and he was seated on a chariot drawn by donkeys. A demoness was flying over him. The sea had dried up, the moon had fallen from the sky, and the earth had been plunged into darkness. Mountains had crashed and the trees had all died. I fear very much that something terrible has happened to my father.'

As he was speaking, the messengers from Ayodhya reached the palace. They saluted the king, and bowed their heads to

Bharata. 'You must return to Ayodhya at once, O prince,' they said to him.

Bharata asked anxiously, 'Is my father well? My mothers, Kaushalya, Sumitra and Kaikeyi? Are Rama and Sita, Lakshmana and Shatrughna in good health?'

But the messengers would not meet his eyes and kept their heads bowed. 'We must return to Ayodhya at once,' was all they would say.

The king of Kakeya ordered his ministers to prepare for Bharata's departure and asked them to prepare valuable gifts for him to take back—horses, jewels, gold coins and baskets of sweets and fruits.

But the prince refused to wait and rode ahead. 'I must reach Ayodhya as soon as I can,' he told his grandfather. 'My heart tells me something is wrong.'

He set off on his fastest horse, reaching Ayodhya as dawn was breaking the following morning. In the summer months, people were usually up and about at this hour, but today there was not a single person to be seen on the streets. The streets, which were always washed clean with scented water, were strewn with dead leaves and broken branches. Sorrow seemed to be in the air.

When Bharata entered the palace, the eerie silence of the jewelled halls made his heart freeze. The court musicians sat as if turned to stone, the fountains in the courtyards were dry, and even the birds seemed to have forgotten how to sing. But no one seemed willing to reply to Bharata's anxious questions about what had happened.

Bharata quickly walked to his father's chambers. The king's bedroom was empty. 'Maybe he is with my mother in her room,' he thought and rushed there.

When he entered the room and saw his mother dressed in white widows' robes, he knew at once what had happened. 'O father, O my king, you have left us!' he cried out, and broke into sobs.

When at last he collected himself somewhat, he wiped his tears and turned to his mother. 'When did this happen? He was not ill, was he? Mother, why did you not send for me?'

Kaikeyi put her arms around her son. 'Calm yourself, my son. You should not grieve so much. He was a father to be proud of, a great king who always did his duty and never broke his word. Now he has gone to live in heaven. Rise, my son. We should also rejoice,' she said, a smile appearing on her face. 'You are king now. This great kingdom with all its wealth is yours to enjoy.'

But Bharata, still wrapped in his grief, did not hear her words. 'I pray to the gods to grant him peace. I must go at once to prepare for mourning. Where is Rama? I must be with my dear brother now to share our grief,' he mumbled as he stood up slowly.

Kaikeyi put her hand out to stop him. Her smile had vanished. She was a little nervous about telling Bharata what had really happened while he was away. 'Wait,' she said quickly. 'Rama is not here. He is roaming in the forest somewhere. Come, let us talk about your coronation ceremony. Imagine, my son—king.'

Bharata was walking towards the door, but he stopped at her words. 'What are you talking about?' he exclaimed. 'Why should I be the king? Why has Rama gone to the forest? Why did he leave my father when he was ill and dying? I do not understand... Where is Lakshmana? I must ask him...' Distress overcame him, and he could speak no more.

Kaikeyi knew that she would have to tell Bharata the truth. She swallowed once and then spoke in a loud voice. 'I asked the king to send Rama to the forest for fourteen years. I asked him to give you the kingdom. The king had granted me two wishes many years ago and, being a man of honour, he could not refuse me. I did this for you, my son. This vast kingdom, this glittering golden palace, this famous city of Ayodhya, this huge army with hundreds of thousands of men, horses and elephants, this treasure house full of gold—all this is yours now. I got it all for you... O king, take it and be happy.' Kaikeyi's voice was full of pride as she finished.

Bharata stepped back from her as if she had slapped him. His face was flushed with anger and he caught hold of his mother's shoulders. 'What are you saying? Have you lost your mind after my father's death? I—king! Rama will become king. He is the oldest. Why do you speak such absurd words?' he cried out in anguish. 'Mother, I cannot believe you said all this. I must go and find Lakshmana. He will know where Rama is.'

'You won't find any of them here. Rama, Lakshmana and Sita have gone to the forest. I told you just now. But forget them! We must speak to the ministers about your coronation,' said Kaikeyi, trying to distract him.

Bharata threw his hands up in the air and began to roar angrily. 'O, what have you done? Do you think I will take this kingdom from my brother? You have killed my father, I know, with this evil deed. You had my brother banished—all for a crown for me, which I do not want! O god of death, why did you not take this woman before she could do such a cruel, wicked thing? I hate to think you are my mother! I hate the thought that I was born from you!'

As his furious voice echoed around the silent palace, everyone cowered in fear lest he draw his sword and kill the queen. But they were also glad in their hearts that Bharata was protesting against this injustice and had not been overcome by greed for the throne, that he was proving himself to be a loyal son and a devoted brother. 'Look, he is rushing out of the palace. What is he going to do?' one palace guard asked another, leaning over the parapet.

That was what the whole city was wondering. Everyone in Ayodhya was very unhappy and worried. Their good and noble king had died, their beloved prince was in the forest somewhere, and now Bharata was charging about the palace like a man who had gone mad with grief.

'We must ask Bharata to accept the crown,' said the ministers, shaking their heads and stroking their beards. 'We cannot leave our kingdom without a king. Enemies will seize this chance and attack our borders. The old king, may the gods grant him peace, is dead. Bharata must become the king.'

When they went to look for Bharata, they found him preparing for a journey. 'Prince, we have come to ask you to accept the crown. Do not delay; it is essential that the kingdom has a king,' said the prime minister, bowing. The other ministers all nodded their agreement. Bharata looked at them, his face angry and sad. 'I will never accept the crown. It belongs to my brother, Rama, and you all know it well. The king wished it, the people of Ayodhya wish it and more than anyone, I wish it. If it had not been for my mother, my father would have been alive and Rama the yuvraj,' he said. 'But do not worry. I am going to the forest to look for Rama. I will bring him back and make him the king. I will leave at once, and this injustice will be put right. Get the army ready. I will escort him back to his coronation with the splendour he deserves.' His voice was so firm that all the ministers scuttled away like scared rabbits.

A cloud of dust rose in the sky and the monkeys in the forest chattered nervously as the huge army began to march towards the forest. Bharata charged ahead on his steed, impatient at every small delay. 'Tell them to clear the roads, make a bridge of boats over the river. We must travel faster!' he commanded, his voice rough with dust.

When the army reached the banks of the river Ganga, they made such a noise with the horses neighing, the elephants trumpeting and the soldiers shouting as they marched that Guha's men, who were watching from the other side of the river, got very frightened. 'We can see the flag of Ayodhya flying on the elephants. What should we do?' they asked Guha.

'Let us wait and watch until they cross the river,' he counselled. 'It must be Bharata. If he has come to fight Rama, we will show him what fighting in our land is about. But if he has come to seek Rama, we will give him all our help.'

When Bharata crossed the river with his army, Guha came to the bank to greet him with gifts as he did with all visiting kings and princes. On discovering that Bharata wanted to take Rama back and make him king, Guha was delighted. He sent his men to once with Bharata to Sage Bharadwaj's ashram, for he had heard that Rama had gone there.

The sage told Bharata to look for Rama in Chitrakoot. As Bharata began his journey deeper into the forest, he left most of his army behind, taking only a few ministers and his brother, Shatrughna, with him.

Lakshmana was guarding the hut at Chitrakoot as usual, when he saw the distant flutter of the flag. 'Look, there is our flag,' he said to Rama. 'There is Bharata coming towards the hill. Do you think he wants to fight us now that he has become the yuvraj?' Lakshmana's eyes were full of rage as he paced up and down. 'I can stop him with just one arrow if you command me.'

Rama looked at him, surprised. 'Why should you stop our brother? I want to meet him. He will bring news of our parents.'

Rama, Lakshmana and Sita stood outside the hut and waited for Bharata and Shatrughna. When Bharata saw Rama standing outside the hut, he started running towards him, pushing his way through the undergrowth, not caring for the thorns that caught at and ripped his clothes and scratched his face. He felt that his heart would break when he saw his brother—a prince of a great noble house—standing outside a grass hut, dressed in bark and deerskin, his hair a tangled, matted mass.

'O Rama, that I have to see you—who should be on the throne, wearing robes of silk and precious jewels—stand before me like this!' cried Bharata to himself as he ran towards his brothers.

Rama walked down the hillside from his hut, followed by Lakshmana, and went to greet his brothers. For a moment, the four brothers stood still together, and it seemed to all those who looked on that a strange golden light emerged from the sky and wrapped itself around them.

Bharata hugged Rama, sobbing loudly. 'Please forgive me, Rama, for the pain my mother has caused you. I beg you to return at once to Ayodhya and take your place on the throne of a kingdom that is rightfully yours.'

Rama put his hand on his brother's head and gently patted him. 'Do not make yourself so unhappy. I do not know what Mother Kaikeyi has to do with this. I came here because our father asked me to, and that is also why I have to remain here. We must both obey our father's wishes.'

Bharata, unable to give his brothers the news of King Dashrath's death, stayed where he was, sobbing. It was left to Shatrughna to speak. 'Rama, Lakshmana,' he said slowly. 'I would give anything not to be the bearer of such tidings, but...'

He broke off and was silent. After a while, he continued again. 'Our father is no more, my brothers. The pain of your departure was too much for him.'

Rama stood very still, his face as if carved out of stone. Lakshmana sat down on the forest floor and covered his face. Their grief was so deep that they could not even cry.

After a long while, Bharata spoke. 'Our father is no more. Your promise to him is no longer binding. Come back and be king. The kingdom needs you.'

But Rama would not agree. A promise was a promise, he said, and he would not return until fourteen years had elapsed. 'Bharata, you must return to Ayodhya and be a great king, like our father,' he said.

But this time Bharata would not agree. Like a child he begged Rama to come back. 'I will stay in the forest instead,' he offered.

His brothers argued with him long and hard, but Rama's quiet resolve was not to be shaken. His father's word was of utmost importance to him, especially now that he was no more.

Finally, Bharata had to accept that Rama would not go back, and that he had to fulfil his responsibility and rule the kingdom. 'I will rule,' he said, 'but only in your name. Please give me your sandals. I will place them on the throne and there they will stay until you return so that people never forget who the true king is. I will make sure that our kingdom is safe, but I will not be king. And I will not live in the palace, but in a little village hut such as yours until you come back and take back your kingdom.'

Rama was touched by his brother's devotion and put his arms around him.

They sat quietly for a long time, the four brothers and Sita, thinking of all that had happened to them in the last few days. Finally, in the company of their closest ones, the brothers could break down and weep for the father they had all loved so much. As they spoke, they realized how their lives had changed beyond measure. It was barely a week ago that Rama had been trying on his lavish coronation robes, and now he was clad in bark. Bharata, who had never thought that he would have to take on such responsibility, was going to be king. And the most difficult of all was the realization that they now had no father to turn to, whose wisdom would guide them. They were now men who had to make all their decisions themselves. As the sun set, they made the most of what they knew would be their last hour together for many years to come.

When Bharata returned to Ayodhya, he placed Rama's sandals on the throne. 'He is the true king, I am merely his deputy while he is away,' he declared in court. A white silk umbrella was held over the sandals at all times. Bharata knew it was strange, but when he was sad or lonely, he would secretly go and sit near the sandals to feel his brother's presence.

Everyone in the palace shunned Kaikeyi, especially the son for whom she had done all her evil. Manthara was hated by all, and seldom seen during the day.

Into the Wild

Rama decided to move deeper into the forest after Bharata left. Though they had a comfortable hut and Sita had made a pretty garden of fruit and flowering plants, he felt that they had been found too easily by the people from Ayodhya. Also, because they had heard of Dashrath's death while living there, the hut had become a place full of sadness. He felt restless, and believed that it was time to start again in a new place.

They left Chitrakoot and began their journey further into the forest. As they walked, the paths became narrower and narrower, and soon they were stumbling over stones and thorny shrubs. The forest was so dense and dark that sometimes they could barely see where they were going. The trees grew very high and were covered with strange flowers that they had never seen before.

From somewhere far away came the sounds of tigers roaring and wolves howling. They were now in what was a part of the forest of Dandaka, where Rama and Lakshmana had once come to kill Tataka. Though the forest had become a different place after she was killed, a sense of darkness lingered. Some strange beings, Tataka's old followers, still hid in the shadows. The three of them walked silently, staying together at all times. Rama looked around him with alert eyes while Lakshmana kept his hand on the bow constantly. Sita did not like this forest with its eerie sounds and strange flowers, and kept close to Rama.

Suddenly, with no warning, a huge demon emerged out of the green shadows. He was covered with the entrails of dead animals and blood dripped from his mouth and all over his matted fur. He roared as he charged towards them.

Sita stood bravely as Rama and Lakshmana sent a shower of arrows towards the giant. Though some hit him, nothing seemed to slow him down. When he came close to them, the monster stopped in his charge and laughed at them. 'Ha ha, pretty little ones, come on! Shoot me! No weapon can harm Viradhha,' he taunted.

Rama sent another arrow which pierced the demon's heart and came out dripping in blood. But the demon still stomped around, completely unaffected. Rama and Lakshmana shot so many arrows into Viradhha's head, stomach, arms and legs that he began to look like a giant porcupine. Though he howled with pain, he did not seem to become weaker.

Finally, one of the arrows hit him between the eyes and, losing his balance, the demon fell over. Rama jumped forward at once, and before Viradhha could recover, placed his foot on his mighty throat. With a flash of light, the demon disappeared and a handsome young man with a kind face stood where his body had lain.

'You have saved me,' he said in a gentle voice, smiling gratefully at Rama and Lakshmana. 'I was once a gandharva and lived in heaven, but I was cursed to become a demon and sent to this dreadful forest as punishment. Now, my lords, you have freed me!' His voice was joyous, and he flew away to heaven, humming a song which they could hear for a long time.

Rama, Lakshmana and Sita began walking again. They climbed over hills and walked through valleys, and crossed streams and passed lakes where hundreds of lotuses grew. Waterbirds swimming in the lakes with their young, and herds of deer grazing watched them as they passed.

The forest was always full of surprises. Sometimes it was dark and dense, but when they turned a corner it would clear suddenly and they would find themselves in a pretty meadow full of flowers and berries. They drank water from the springs, rested at night in the shelter of the huge branches of old trees, and ate whatever fruits, roots and berries they found. Sometimes they found one of the remote ashrams that dotted the forest, where rishis lived a life of meditation and prayer, and they would stay there for a while, talking and praying with the rishis.

Time passed slowly but happily. Sita could hardly remember her old life in the palace. The soft bed she had slept on, the silken robes and jewels she had worn, the delicious food that the palace cooks had served her, and the fun she used to have with her friends—all seemed very far away and unreal. The forest was now her home, and she was happy here for she got to spend so much more time with her husband.

Ten years rolled by, almost without their realizing the passage of time. Rama, Lakshmana and Sita lived quietly, either on their own or sometimes with the rishis in different ashrams. Sometimes they stayed for as little as one week, sometimes they lingered on for a year. Their presence made the rishis very happy. 'When you are with us, our troubles disappear like mist before the rising sun and we can pray in peace. No demon or evil spirit dares come near our ashram,' they said. Sometimes, at their request, Rama and Lakshmana went out to kill the fierce demons who plagued various ashrams.

And thus the years passed. Rama, Lakshmana and Sita all changed as time went by. They were no longer the youths who had set out. The rishis had taught them much about meditation and prayer, and they were now stronger in spirit as well as in body. When they had set out from Ayodhya, the only world they had known was that of the palace. Now they knew so much more of how other people lived. They had acquired much knowledge through their conversations with the wise sages, both of the material world and of that of the spirit. They learnt by living in close association with nature how she moved in mysterious but wonderful cycles, and how life itself had so many richer things to offer than they had ever known before.

In all these years, they had become used to the uneven paths, the thorny bushes, and the insects and snakes that lay on their paths. They were not afraid of these any more, for they realized that the creatures of the wild do not attack unless they are provoked. They loved to see the many beautiful things—the bright flowers with their soothing fragrances, the sweet fruits, and the pretty wings of the colourful butterflies that flitted across their faces. The deer always came up to Sita as she walked, and usually naughty monkeys followed them, chattering merrily. They enjoyed every part of the forest.

There were always so many new things to see, new birds and beasts to meet. They learnt how to make medicines from plants, and they heard stranger tales of wonderful new lands from travellers they met.

Years passed, the seasons changed the colours of the forest from green to gold and then green again. Seedlings grew into tall trees as old trees fell away. Their old friends— newborn elephants, deer and tigers—now had offspring of their own.

Finally, after more than ten years of wandering, Rama, Lakshmana and Sita came to the river Godavari. On the banks of this river stood Sage Agastya's ashram.

Panchavati

Sage Agastya was famous, both in heaven and on earth, because of his great powers. When Rama and Lakshmana were growing up, they had heard many stories of his amazing powers. As they walked towards Agastya's ashram, they told Sita these stories.

'Sage Agastya can even make mountains bow to him,' said Rama. 'Once the Vindhya mountains began growing steadily towards heaven and threatened to block the sun's journey across the sky. The gods had grown worried and asked Agastya for help. The sage walked up to the mountains, which bowed low to greet him. "Bless you. May you remain like this till I return from my journey," the sage said as he departed. He has never gone back and the Vindhya mountains remain low to this day, waiting for his return.'

'The sage had also outwitted two demons,' said Lakshmana, laughing. 'Vaataapi and Ilvala loved eating humans and they had made a cunning plan to get their meals easily. Vaataapi had a special boon given to him which made it impossible to kill him. He could be slaughtered, chopped up, hacked and sliced into tiny pieces. But, thanks to this boon, all the parts would rejoin and Vaataapi would become whole again.

'Ilvala would disguise himself as a Brahmin and go to an ashram. There he would humbly request one of the rishis to come and have a meal at his hut. The rishis were kind people and thought it was rude to refuse. Each day's victim would go with Ilvala and the demon would serve him a delicious meal. The poor rishi would eat it happily, not knowing that it was the demon Vaataapi, cooked with many spices. Once the rishi had finished eating, Ilvala would wait for a few minutes and then shout, "Vaataapi! Vaataapi! Come out." Before the unsuspecting rishi could say or do anything, his stomach would burst as the demon re-formed himself and came charging out. The two demon brothers would then sit down and devour the rishi.

'But when they invited Agastya, the trick did not work. Agastya ate what was served to him and sat back contentedly. "Come out, Vaataapi! Come out!" Ilvala kept shouting, but nothing happened. The sage, with his great powers, had digested the demon. "You have killed my brother ... I will eat you up!" hollered Ilvala, but the sage just gave him an angry look which reduced him to ashes.'

As Lakshmana finished this story, they arrived at the ashram gates. The sage was waiting for him. 'I knew you would come today. The end of your fourteen-year exile is drawing near. You must stay here in my ashram for the remaining period,' said the sage.

Rama thanked him for his kind words but said that they wanted to go deeper into the forest, where there were very few people.

'You can go to Panchavati, which is very beautiful. I will gift you some weapons, which you will need as there are many demons in that part of the forest,' said the sage. He gave them a sword with a sliver blade, two magic quivers from which arrows would never run out, and a magnificent bow made of gold and precious jewels. He also gave Rama a suit of armour which could never be pierced. Then he blessed them and told them how to get to Panchavati through secret forest paths.

Once more, the three of them set out into the forest, walking through the dense jungle. They walked in a companionable silence, enjoying the beauty around them.

'Look! There is a huge creature on the banyan tree. Stay here, Sita, it might attack us,' said Lakshmana suddenly. What he saw was a giant eagle perched on an old tree, but he suspected that it might be a demon that had cleverly disguised itself as an eagle.

The old eagle lifted its head and bowed to them. 'Children, come to me. I am so happy to see you,' he said in a weak voice.

'Who are you, sir?' asked Rama politely.

'I am Jatayu. I was a friend of your father's—he was a noble king indeed. Come, sit down and listen to my story, young princes.' He shifted himself along the branch to a more comfortable position, and then fluffing up his feathers and shutting his eyes, he began his tale in a sing-song voice.

'First let me introduce myself properly. I have descended from a noble line of kings. My mother, Vinata, came from the house of Daksha, my great-aunts are the mothers of lions and langurs, waterbirds and pheasants, elephants and hooded serpents. These fruit trees you see around you are gifts from my mother's family.

'Once when I was very young, my brother, Sampati, and I decided to race each other. "Let us see who reaches the sun first," said my brother, who was always very adventurous. So we began to fly towards the sun. I was racing ahead, thrilled to be flying at such a great speed through the sky, and before I knew it, I had entered the sun's orbit. There was a flash of fire and my wings began to burn. I did not know what to do and thought my end was near.

'Just then Sampati flew above my head and spread his wings out to protect me from the sun's fiery rays. Alas, he got badly burnt trying to save me and fell from the sky. I have never found him again. The birds in the forest tell me they have seen him living at an ashram far away from here.'

There was silence when he finished. The sadness in the old bird's voice brought tears to Sita's eyes. She knew how sad it was to be parted from one's own family. She at least had her husband and dear brother-in-law, but this old bird had no one. She put her hand out and stroked the faded feathers.

The old bird smiled. 'You have nothing to worry about, my child. Though it is dangerous in this forest, I will always be there to protect you, even if it costs me my life.' Jatayu flapped his huge wings slowly as he spoke.

Rama, Lakshmana and Sita thanked him and walked on, wondering how the poor old bird could save anyone. But Jatayu knew that soon a day would come when he would have to fight to the death to save Sita, so he shut his eyes once more and folded his wings, waiting for the last and final battle of his long life.

The path began to climb up as Rama, Lakshmana and Sita walked, and soon they came to a beautiful hilly area. The air was cool and fresh, and there was a fragrance of roses in the breeze. They could see a river glistening around the hill and herds of deer were drinking water on its banks. Sal, date palm, jackfruit, kadam, mango, sandalwood and flame of the forest grew in abundance. Shrubs of jasmine and rose bushes surrounded the grassy meadows.

'This is where we should live for the rest of the time we have to spend in the forest,' said Rama, and Lakshmana and Sita agreed.

'I will build the hut all by myself,' said Lakshmana. Rama and Sita started to protest, but Lakshmana said, 'I learnt a new way of building a hut, and I want to show you how it is done.' They laughed and agreed. In all these years of living in the forest, Lakshmana had learnt how to build better and more comfortable huts. Though as a prince he had been trained only in warfare and kingly duties, he had taught himself every skill needed to survive in the wild and was constantly surprising them with new tricks.

Lakshmana set out to gather materials for building the hut. He found plenty of hardwood nearby, along with bamboo and grass. Rama and Sita sat in the shade of a mango tree and watched with wonder as Lakshmana worked.

First, he built walls out of the wet earth he dug up. Then he added sturdy pillars using hardwood branches. On top of this structure, he laid a row of bamboo sticks in a criss-cross pattern. On this framework, he put smaller branches to make the roof stronger, and tied them down with a rope he had made out of fine bark. Finally, he spread a layer of soft grass and large leaves to make a waterproof roof for the hut. He even shaped a veranda of wet earth in front of the hut with a step, and made a railing of thin twigs all around it. Rama and Sita applauded in delight. This was the prettiest hut he had ever built.

Life in Panchavati was peaceful and happy. First thing every morning, the three of them would bathe in the river Godavari, gather lotus buds and offer prayers to the sun god. Then they would drink the fresh cool water from the spring and eat whatever fruits or berries they had gathered. There was the hut to tend to, and animals to look after and play with. All day long they would walk in the shadows or sit in their pretty hut and talk about ideas and beliefs that the rishis had discussed with them or about their loved ones. Rama spoke kindly about Queen Kaikeyi, too, and always checked Lakshmana when he tried to say harsh words about what she had done. In the evening they would walk by the river and watch the magic of twilight.

The seasons passed, and soon it was spring. Trees changed from brown to green again; new fruits and flowers appeared. The family of deer which had been adopted by Sita had a new brood of fawns, and the peacocks, too, brought a dozen new chicks to the hut. Sita happily fed them tender shoots of grass and freshly gathered rosebuds.

But this peaceful life was not to last, for evil eyes watched them from the darkness of the forest.

Soorpanakha

Soorpanakha was a demoness who often roamed this part of the forest, hunting for wild animals to eat. When she saw Rama sitting outside his hut one day, she fell in love with him at once.

'O, what a handsome man,' she said to herself. 'I never knew humans could be so wonderful looking. I must marry him.' She transformed herself into a beautiful woman and glided up to the step in front of the hut where Rama was sitting.

'Please let me introduce myself,' she said, simpering and speaking in a cooing voice. 'I am Princess Soorpanakha, sister of the great king of Lanka, Ravana. I wish to marry you and take you back to Lanka with me. You will live with me like a prince and have all the pleasures you want.' She fluttered her eyelashes as she spoke.

Rama was surprised, but he smiled at her and spoke gently. 'No, lady, I cannot marry you. You see, I already have a wife.' He pointed to where Sita was pruning a rose bush nearby.

'What! That skinny creature is not fit for you. I am the one who should be your wife, you handsome man.' She flashed him a coy smile.

'No, no, that is not possible. Look, there is my brother, who is more handsome than I am. Marry him,' said Rama, laughing.

Soorpanakha turned her eyes towards Lakshmana. Yes, he was quite handsome, too, as he stood laughing at this exchange. 'All right,' she said. 'You may marry me. Come let us go.'

She laid a hand on his arm, but Lakshmana pushed her away. 'No, thank you. I have no wish to be married,' he said with a naughty smile.

Suddenly Soorpanakha lost her temper. 'I will eat up this creature who is your wife,' she shouted, turning to Rama. 'Then you can marry me!' She reached out to grab Sita's hand. Her beautiful face turned into an ugly mask and her hands sprouted into claws.

Rama realized instantly that she was a demoness and sprang up. 'Lakshmana, deal with her while I take Sita into the hut,' he said in an angry voice.

Lakshmana was furious with this woman who had attacked his gentle sister-in-law. With a lightning movement of his sword he cut off Soorpanakha's nose and the tips of her long hairy ears.

Howling with pain as blood dripped from her face, the demoness ran into the forest. 'I will tell my brothers and you will see what happens. I will make you pay for this insult,' she screamed as she ran. Her horrible voice frightened all the creatures of the forest, and shattered the peace and quiet of Panchavati.

Though they did not know it then, her scream also marked the end of the peaceful rhythm of their days together, for this was the beginning of a long period of turmoil, during which Rama would have to fight many battles and Sita would have to suffer quietly.

Khara's Revenge

Screaming and screeching, Soorpanakha crashed through the trees, frightening all the birds and animals. 'Revenge, revenge,

revenge,' she chanted in a voice which boomed all over the forest. 'I will drink their blood. I will crush their bones into a pulp,' she yelled, leaping over the treetops like a giant frog. 'How dare these humans insult me—a princess of royal demon blood!' Soorpanakha grew bigger and bigger as her rage bubbled and simmered, and soon she was like a volcano spewing blood, smoke and fire.

When she arrived at the forest hideout of her brother Khara, all the demons were shocked to see her in such a terrible state. Khara, one of the most powerful of all the demon-warriors, could not believe this noseless, earless, tearful being was his little sister.

'Who has done this to you?' he roared, stroking her matted hair. 'My poor sister, your pretty nose chopped off! Tell me and I will make him into food for the vultures!'

Soorpanakha told him, between loud sobs, her own version of what had happened. 'I was wandering in the forest when I saw these three humans. I went up to ask them what they were doing in our forest—your forest where no human dares to enter. But as soon as they saw me, they chopped off my nose, my ears... Oooooo! How it hurts, brother!' she howled in dismay. 'Just two frail humans, but see what they have done to your sister! You must punish them. You must take revenge on our behalf. You must save our honour and that of the entire demon race!' Her yelps of pain and glares of fury as she jumped up and down made the other demons back away.

Khara rose and began barking orders to his generals. 'Go at once. Take some of our most ferocious demons and finish off these humans. Wipe the grass with their broken heads and limbs. I do not want any humans roaming about in my forest. This is the sanctuary of the demons!'

Fourteen huge demons set out at once to kill Rama and Lakshmana as revenge for their attack on the demoness. Soorpanakha went with them to show them the way.

They found the two brothers sitting quietly in front of the hut, Sita by their side. But the brothers, who had suspected that Soorpanakha would come back, had their bows and arrows with them.

'There they are,' hissed Soorpanakha, pointing a claw at them. 'Kill them and give me their blood to drink.'

At first, the demons laughed when they saw how small the two brothers were compared to them. 'Ha ha, two little sparrows! Why did fourteen of us waste our time? Let me stun them with one slap, then a quick knock with my club to smash their tiny heads,' roared one.

But even as he spoke, Lakshmana neatly sliced his head off with a single arrow. Then one by one, all the other thirteen demons were quickly and quietly killed by Rama and Lakshmana.

Soorpanakha was shocked into silence at first. Then she flew into a terrible rage which made her bloat until she was as big as a thundercloud. Long before she reached his hideout, Khara could hear her shrill cries which disrupted his enjoyment as he sat dining on a whole buffalo.

'Now what happened?' he asked irritably as soon as she arrived.

'What happened?' screeched Soorpanakha. 'Fourteen of your mightiest demons are lying dead, killed by the same humans who chopped off my nose and ear.'

Khara was sure she was making a mistake—maybe she was going mad, he thought—but decided to go see for himself.

When Soorpanakha heard him say that he would go at once, she flew to him. 'No, do not go alone. I beg of you, take your army. Those brothers are like baby cobras—small but deadly. Please do not go alone!'

Khara was amused to hear this, but as he did not want to agitate his sister any more, he commanded his army to come with him. Fourteen thousand demons, armed with spears, clubs, swords and nooses, marched through the forests, creating such a terrible racket that the birds flew back to their nests and animals hid, even though it was daylight.

'What is happening in our forest today?' the ground animals asked the birds with their superior vantage points. 'First that demoness with no ears or nose came charging through, then came fourteen demons who never returned and now this huge army.' The worried birds shook their heads and told the mongoose, hares, squirrels and snakes to hide their young. They themselves buried their heads in their nests, hoping the army would not break the branches of their trees.

As the army marched on, creating a path through the forest, evil omens began to appear. A black circle hid the sun and crimson clouds floated in the sky. Soon big, fat drops of red rain began to fall on the heads of the marching demons. When they looked up, there was a vulture perched on their banner.

But Khara was not worried about these evil signs. 'It is very foolish to take such a huge army to kill just two humans,' he grumbled, wiping a red raindrop from his nose. 'Sisters!'

Rama and Lakshmana saw the army coming towards them, but they were not afraid. They had killed many demons in their years in the forest. Though they had never faced such a huge army, they had great faith in their own abilities. 'I knew the demoness would do something like this. Lakshmana, take Sita to a safe place where no arrows can harm her. I will deal with this demon-army,' said Rama, lifting his bow.

But before he pulled an arrow out of the quiver, he spoke to Khara, as this was the correct thing for a prince to do before launching an attack on the enemy. 'Stop and reconsider before you attack us, O warrior. We were living here peacefully before the demoness attacked my wife. State what you want from us and I shall not harm you.'

Khara gave a roar of anger when he heard this fragile human stand before his mighty army and speak to him in this way. 'I will crush your bones; I will drink your blood,' he yelled, his eyes filled with rage, forgetting all about princely speeches. He ordered his army to charge.

In huge waves, they came at Rama, but not a single demon could touch him. With hands as swift as a falcon's wings, he sent a shower of arrows to cut them down before they could even come near him. Rama's arrows struck at the demons like a swarm of bees, destroying the vast army before the sun set over the trees.

Soon Khara and all his fourteen thousand demons, except for one, were lying dead on the forest floor. After all was finally quiet, the creatures of the forest crept out of their hiding places to gaze at the fallen demons and rejoice that Rama had cleared the forest of the demons who preyed on them.

The gods, who were watching Rama's battle with the demons, exclaimed amongst themselves. They had never imagined a mortal man could be capable of such valour. And they too rejoiced at his prowess, for they knew that soon there would be an even more deadly battle that Rama would have to fight, where he would fulfil the destiny for which he had been born.

In Ravana's Court

Through the dimly lit forest ran one dark figure, crying with pain, his demon face scarred with arrows. This was Akampana, who had hidden behind a tree and managed to survive despite being hit by Rama's arrows.

He ran all day and all night for many days, until he reached the shore and then took a flying jump over the sea to reach Lanka at dawn. He stood before his king, trembling with fear, because he knew Ravana was going to be furious.

'O king, I bring terrible news. Your brother Khara is dead; all your brave generals are lying dead on the forest floor. The entire unit of your army that was commanded by Khara has been slaughtered. I do not know...' whispered Akampana and then fell down unconscious at Ravana's feet.

The king of demons rose, his mighty body shaking with fury. He was enormously tall, with ten heads which could look in every direction. His twenty black eyes flashed and crackled like lightning. His huge body was marked with battle scars and when he spoke, it was like thunder rumbling.

Ravana believed that he was the most powerful king in heaven, on earth or in the netherworld. Over the years he had defeated all the gods and demons who stood in his way. He had done years of penance and had received many boons, including one from Brahma which had made it impossible for any demon or god to defeat him in battle. He was a great warrior, learned in ancient texts, and ruled over the vast and rich kingdom of Lanka.

Lanka was a land of fabled splendour. Ravana's palace was made of solid gold, with diamond and ruby pillars and emerald-studded walls. The throne he sat on was carved out of a gold block and his main crown was set with a row of huge diamonds, each as large as a rock. Unlike other kings, he needed not just one crown but ten, and each one was lavishly decorated with rubies, diamonds, sapphires, emeralds and pearls which he had stolen from the gods.

Though Ravana was a powerful king, he was not a well-loved one. The demons of Lanka feared him for he was neither just nor noble. He was selfish and proud, and did not care about his fellow demons.

As Akampana lay still near his feet, Ravana rose from his throne and kicked him, growling viciously like an angry tiger. 'Who has done this?' he roared, and all the demons in the palace began to shake with fear. 'I will destroy the god or demon who has killed my brother. Let him take just one last breath. I will break his head and grind his bones under my feet. Just show me who it is,' he barked, his twenty eyes flashing with fury.

'It was no demon or god who killed your brother and maimed your sister,' screeched Soorpanakha, as she hobbled into the palace, dripping blood on the golden floor. All the demons were shocked to see her mutilated face with her nose and ears chopped off.

She stood in front of the throne and looked up at Ravana. Her mind was working quickly. Her love for Rama had now become the most bitter hatred, and she wanted more than anything to see him dead. She knew Ravana was the only person who could take revenge on him. 'Look at me, O great king of Lanka. Look at your poor sister and listen to her sad tale,' she began piteously. 'She stands in front of you, with her ears and nose cut off. Your brother, the great demon-general, lies dead on the forest floor along with fourteen thousand of your best soldiers. Yet you sit happily on your throne, surrounded by your beautiful wives... You, who is the greatest of all warriors, greatest of all kings, do not know what shame has been brought upon your name by an ordinary human. O Ravana, my brother, you may have defeated all the gods in heaven and the demons in hell, but a frail man by the name of Rama has shown to everyone that you are nothing compared to him.'

The king of demons remained silent. He was so angry at his sister's mocking words that he wanted to kill her then and there, but he controlled himself because killing women or demonesses was not the right thing to do for a great warrior like himself.

But Soorpanakha went on and on, taunting him, making sure all the demons around them heard her words. 'I have seen Rama, and now I know who is mightier. You may be a great warrior, but you are no match for Rama. He will cut off all your heads with just one arrow. He has his brother with him, who is also a very strong man. The two of them can finish our entire army. You could have asked our poor brother Khara, but alas, he lies dead, killed by Rama's arrow.'

Seeing the fury in Ravana's eyes, Soorpanakha decided to change her tune. She began talking about Sita. 'This Rama, he has the most exquisite wife in the world. How beautiful she is! Like a lotus which blooms only in heaven. When I saw her, I thought at once that she would make a perfect wife for you. O dear brother, I went to them only to bring Sita to you, but see what happened to me!' Seeing that the angry gleam had left Ravana's eyes, she went back to her earlier theme. 'If only you were as strong as Rama… Who will I ask for revenge and protection; there is no one who can help me,' she ended wailing and beating her chest.

Ravana stormed out of the great hall, but his sister's mocking voice seemed to follow him everywhere. The chambers echoed with taunts, and voices jeered at him from behind every pillar. Ravana grew more and more angry, but he was a very clever demon and did not allow his anger to overpower his judgement.

'I will not rush out and defeat this Rama, though I can do it very easily. I am the greatest warrior in the three worlds. There is no need to prove it. But I should take revenge for the attack on my sister. I will carry off Rama's wife. That will harm him more,' he thought as he paced up and down, all his heads clear and cool. 'But how should I do this?'

After a while, an idea struck him. 'I will ask my uncle Mareecha for some magic that will help me abduct this beautiful Sita. If she is as gorgeous as my sister says, then her husband will surely die pining for her,' he muttered, his black eyes gleaming with evil, and plans swirling in his mind.

Mareecha

Ravana ordered his chariot to be brought out. The shining golden chariot appeared within moments, as if by magic. Pulled by six mules with tangled mane and fiery eyes, the chariot could fly, sail or run according to Ravana's wishes. It was the fastest and most beautiful vehicle in heaven, and Ravana had stolen it from Kuber, the god of wealth.

The chariot rose high into the sky as soon as Ravana stepped into it. 'To my uncle, Mareecha,' he ordered, and lashed the mules with a sliver whip to make them go as fast as they could. Riding the winds, facing the sun, they sailed over fields of wheat and dense forests, and crossed raging rivers. Finally, they slowed down to hover over a grassy meadow, and landed near a clump of trees. This was where his uncle, the famous demon-magician, lived.

Mareecha was once a fierce demon who ate humans and animals for breakfast. But after a battle with Rama who had hurled him into the deep sea, Mareecha had given up his wicked ways. He lived peacefully in a hut in this quiet meadow, looking after the birds and animals of the forest.

Mareecha was not pleased to see Ravana's golden chariot land in his fields because he knew his nephew had come to ask him to do some evil deed. 'He would never travel all this way just to ask about my health,' he thought, coming out to meet the king of demons.

Ravana strode into the hut and threw his whip down while his mules stomped outside, all over the flowers that Mareecha had planted near his hut. Mareecha watched them sadly.

'Uncle, you have to do something for me. At once,' said Ravana. He described briefly what had happened. 'I want to take revenge by stealing Rama's wife. You with your great powers of magic will draw Rama away while I...'

Mareecha shook his head sadly. 'Forget this wicked idea. Give up thoughts of revenge. Go back and rule over your kingdom. Rama has done you no wrong; I am sure Soorpanakha is not telling you the whole truth. This plan of yours will only bring death and untold misery for the demons...'

But before he could finish, Ravana had begun to thump his fists on the walls of the hut in fury. 'You will do as I say, uncle. I am your king. I have to take revenge. I have to make these humans suffer. Get into my chariot at once if you value your life.'

Mareecha shut his eyes and sighed. 'It is my destiny to die by the hand of Rama. Once he has spared my life, when he killed Subhahu, but now it is time for me to end my life on this earth. So let it be.'

As the golden chariot raced through the sky, Ravana told Mareecha what he had to do. 'Only you with your great magical powers can carry this plan out. You will turn yourself into a beautiful deer, the most beautiful in the world, and you will show yourself to Sita. She will certainly ask Rama to catch this exquisite animal for her. When Rama follows you into the forest, you must run fast and make sure you lead him into the darkest part of the forest. After that, I will do what I have to do,' Ravana ended with a wicked smile, which spread across all his ten heads. 'Faster,' he yelled, and lashed the mules, making them bray loudly as they raced across the sky, their hearts full of malice.

The Golden Deer

It was a lovely morning. Sita was out in the forest gathering flowers. There were some very pretty white jasmine flowers that bloomed only in the morning, which were her favourites. She liked to put them in an earthen bowl of water for they made the hut smell wonderful.

Rama watched her from the hut as she wandered around the edges of the clearing. 'How fragile and tiny she is, yet so strong!' he thought. 'She never complains about the harsh life we have to lead. When we return to the palace I will take good care of her, and give her whatever her heart desires. The fourteen years are almost over and we can return home soon.'

Sita gathered the flowers in a basket made of leaves; their lovely scent filled her with joy. 'How happy our life is here,' she said to herself. 'None of the complications of palace life, no responsibilities.' She smiled gently to herself, unaware of the dark, evil eyes watching her from the forest.

Just as Sita turned to go back to the hut where Rama was waiting for her, she saw the golden deer from the corner of her eyes. She swung around to gaze at it, dropping her basket in amazement. 'Look, oh look!' she cried out in wonder, pointing to it as it pranced around the edges of the clearing behind the hut.

Rama and Lakshmana were surprised to hear Sita call out so loudly and they came out at once, their bows in their hands. They looked at the deer she was pointing at. 'I have never seen anything so beautiful,' cried Sita. 'It must be a creature from heaven, such golden skin, such silver horns.'

The golden deer came towards them, looking as if it wanted to speak to them. Then it skipped away in a flash of shining colour.

All the other deer who came to graze in the clearing moved away, as if they sensed that there was something wrong. But Rama, Lakshmana and Sita did not notice as they were busy watching the golden deer as it ran about, leaping gracefully over the flowers and bushes so that the light glittered on its bright coat. Sometimes it would turn its head to look at Sita, and then dart away.

'Please catch this beautiful deer for me. I will keep it as a pet, and take it back to Ayodhya with me... Please get it for me,' said Sita, turning towards Rama, her eyes full of joy.

The golden deer came very close to them, as if it had heard Sita's wish. It stood for a moment near Sita, but when she reached her hand out to touch it, it jumped away and disappeared into the forest. They could see flashes of gold glinting through the trees.

'I will get the deer for you, my beloved. I will catch it and bring it for you,' said Rama.

Lakshmana looked around the clearing with a frown. 'I do not think you should follow the deer. It may be a trick the demons are playing on us. That deer was not real. I just noticed that the other animals have all moved away from here as if they were afraid. Maybe they can see that it is dangerous.'

Sita was very upset when she heard Lakshmana. 'Of course it is not a demon; it is so pretty. But if you think it is dangerous, don't go.' She tried very hard not to sound disappointed.

Rama was touched that she was so willing to give up what she wanted. 'I will go at once. Do not worry, Lakshmana. If it is a demon, I will kill it. If it is real, I will get it for Sita. You stay here with her,' he said, and quickly ran into the forest.

The deer was waiting for him a little way ahead. It began to skip and run as soon as it saw Rama. Then it stopped to look back. It waited for a few moments, standing still as the sun lit up the sliver spots on its golden body. It seemed to be waiting for Rama to catch up. As soon as Rama came closer, it bowed its glittering horns and raced ahead.

Playing hide-and-seek like this, the magical deer led Rama deep into the dark forest where the trees grew so tall that they blocked out the sunlight, and the grass was blue-black. Rama, focusing on his quarry, did not realize how far into the forest he had come.

Suddenly, the golden deer stood still as if it was tired, and let Rama come up close. Mareecha had played the part his nephew had asked him to and was now waiting for Rama's arrow to pierce his heart. Rama was surprised to see how quietly the deer was standing.

But when Rama reached out to touch it, the deer moved away. This happened a few times. Every time Rama tried to hold it, it moved away a little. But it did not run away. Finally, as if tired of the game, the deer lay down and offered its chest to Rama. It seemed like an invitation to kill it.

'It will not let me catch it, but it wants me to kill it,' thought Rama, amazed. 'Maybe there is some spirit trapped inside it and if I kill it, it will be set free. Maybe it does not want this life any more. I will send an arrow to kill it and take the skin back to Sita.'

He fixed an arrow in his bow and pointed it at the deer. The deer did not try to run away, but its eyes gleamed. It seemed to be encouraging him. Rama shot the arrow, and as it pierced the deer's heart, the animal cried out in a voice that was exactly like Rama's, 'O Lakshmana... O Sita!'

Rama was amazed to hear the deer cry out in his voice. 'Lakshmana was right,' he thought. 'This was no spirit, but a demon. I must go back at once. Sita and Lakshmana will be worried when they hear my voice crying for help.' He began to run back. The path was narrow and his bow clipped the thorny shrubs. The sun had disappeared behind some clouds, and gloom descended quietly and suddenly in the forest, turning the trees into menacing dancing shadows.

When Lakshmana and Sita heard Rama's voice, they were startled. 'Why is he calling in that helpless voice? He can fight anyone single-handedly!' said Lakshmana, worried and tense.

Sita's heart filled with fear, though she tried not to show it. 'Go at once and help him,' she said quietly. 'Something terrible may have happened to him.'

Lakshmana stood on the steps of the hut, unsure of what to do. He did not want to leave Sita alone. 'Rama has asked me to stay here with you. It is my duty to protect you,' he said.

Sita suddenly began to cry loudly. 'Go, go... Save your brother!'

Lakshmana stood still, not knowing what to do.

Sita wept. 'Go, if you love him. Maybe you do not love him! O, if I were a man and could do something to help my lord.' She began calling out to the animals of the forest. 'Please save my Rama, for there is no one else who can. O, what a terrible fate to have a brother who will leave you to die in the forest!'

Finally, Lakshmana could not bear her reproaches any more. 'I am going into the forest, dear sister-in-law.' He thought quickly. 'I will draw you a magic circle. As long as you are in it, you will be safe.'

With the tip of his arrow, he drew a circle in the wet earth all around the hut. He took up his bow and quiver, and turned to Sita as he left. 'Please stay inside the hut, and on no account step outside this circle I have drawn. You will be safe as long as you are inside it,' he said. Then with a heavy heart he set out for the forest to look for Rama.

Sita was left all alone on the veranda in front of the hut, her eyes on the path down which Rama and Lakshmana had disappeared. Tears streamed down her face and her tiny hands were curled into tight fists. The morning, which had been so beautiful just a little while ago, suddenly seemed dark and gloomy. A strange grey-black cloud appeared above the hut, frightening the birds and small forest creatures into silence. 'How quiet the forest is suddenly,' she thought, her heart racing with fear. 'It is as if I am all alone in the whole world.'

The Abduction

But Sita was not alone. From the dark shadows of the forest twenty black eyes watched her. Ravana had been waiting for a long time for this moment, and now finally Sita was alone.

He stepped forward, swiftly changing his huge body, discarding his ten heads, his glittering crowns, his jewels and weapons as he walked. By the time he had reached the hut, the mighty king of demons was a frail, old holy man dressed in saffron robes.

'Pray, kind lady, will you give alms to a hermit?' he said in a soft voice, his eyelids lowered over eyes that gleamed with wickedness.

Sita was not surprised to see a holy man in front of their hut. They often passed by on their way from one ashram to another. She bowed her head and said, 'Please wait for a moment. I will bring you some fruit, sir. That is all we have.' She went into the hut and brought some berries and other fruits on a leaf-plate. She placed them on the step in front of the hut and went in again.

Ravana stood still. It was as if he had been struck by lightning. His heart was racing as it had never done before, his hands trembling. 'How beautiful she is! Like a rare lotus from heaven's lake, like a jewel which only gods can possess. I must make her my wife,' he thought, blood rushing to his head.

He stepped forward and spoke in his gentle voice. 'Why do you leave the food for me outside like this? Will you not give it in my hands, gentle lady?' His voice sounded honey-sweet.

Sita hesitated. She was afraid that she had hurt the holy man's feelings by placing the fruit on the step. She hated to wound a hermit, now that she knew how gentle and kind most of them were. It seemed foolish to be so wary in the middle of the forest. And the hermit seemed like a gentle old man. She felt guilty for being so rude, and picking up the plate, she walked down the single step, over the line that Lakshmana had drawn and reached out to give the man the fruit.

Thunder and lightning came crashing down the moment her foot crossed the line. The circle itself burst into flames. Sita, very frightened now, tried to step back, but the hermit stepped forward and grabbed her hand. As he touched her, his disguise disappeared and the king of demons towered over her, his ten heads dancing like hooded cobras.

'Behold me, beautiful woman,' he roared. 'I am the king of demons, the greatest of all warriors in the three worlds. Henceforth, you belong to me.'

Sita cowered with fear, her eyes blinded by the gold and diamonds of Ravana's opulent necklace glinting in the sudden harsh sunlight. She tried to shout for help but her voice was frozen. With all the strength she had, she tried to pull herself away, but Ravana, who held her tightly with one hand, did not even seem to notice her struggles. With his other hand, he stroked her hair.

'How lovely you are! I shall make you my wife,' he said, his voice suddenly gentle. 'I am the most powerful king in heaven and on earth, richer than the gods and stronger than the demons. The sun cools its rays before me and the sea subsides when I glance at it.' Then he bellowed, his twenty eyes flashing with pride and greed. 'You shall be my queen. Your husband, Rama, is nothing compared to me.'

Sita had been frightened beyond all thought by this demon, but her courage returned when he spoke rudely about her husband. She lifted her head high and said in a trembling voice, trying to sound scornful, 'Sir, do not speak about my lord thus. He is the most noble, brave and kind man in the universe.'

Ravana shook with laughter. 'So you can talk, too, my pigeon! What good is it to be noble and kind when you have no riches and no kingdom? Look at the way he makes you live in this forest. You should be wearing silk and jewels, not this rough bark. You should step only on feathers, not on this hard ground. You who are a jewel should be the wife of a king; and not just any king, but Ravana, before whom the gods tremble with fear. Come with me to Lanka and you shall live like a queen in joy and splendour!'

Sita pulled back in revulsion and began chanting Rama's name despairingly. Ravana gave a thundering cry of rage. He grabbed her by her hair and began to draw her towards the chariot. Sita struggled helplessly, crying with terror. Ravana threw her on the floor of the chariot, hissing angrily like a snake, and whipped the mules who rose at once into the sky.

'Rama, Rama, help! Help me!' cried Sita, but Rama could not hear her cry. The forest gods heard her, as did the animals and birds who watched in horror, but there was nothing any of them could do.

But there was one being who heard her and rushed to her defence. Jatayu, the old warrior, recognized Sita's voice. He looked up at the sky, squinting, for the golden chariot, glittering like a flame in the sunlight, hurt his old eyes. He smiled sadly, for he knew his final battle had come.

'Sita, wait, I am coming!' he said, and rose into the air slowly. Flapping his huge wings as fast as he could, he flew up towards the swift chariot. 'Stop! Let Sita go,' he shouted hoarsely, hitting against the chariot wheels with his powerful wings.

Ravana turned his heads to see what it was that had lunged against the wheels. He roared with laughter when he saw the old bird trying to stop him. He leaned back and lashed his sliver whip at Jatayu. 'Get away, you stupid old bird, before I cut you into pieces,' he snarled.

Jatayu would not let go. He slapped the chariot over and over again with his wings. The mules, frightened of this giant bird, began to bray and slow down. Jatayu swooped forward and scratched Ravana's arms with his claws, drawing blood. Maddened with rage, Ravana shouted and drew out his sword. But his swipes at his enemy were futile, for Jatayu dodged swiftly and then moved in again to attack. With powerful swipes of his wings, he knocked one wheel off the chariot.

But the old bird knew that his strength was fast running out and he could not fight much longer. So he tried to reason with Ravana. 'Stop, O king of demons. Let Sita go. How can such a great warrior behave like a coward and a thief? Steal another man's wife? Sita is the daughter of a king and the wife of the future king of Ayodhya. This shameful deed will only bring death and destruction upon you.'

Ravana paid no heed to Jatayu's words, but seeing that he was breathless after his speech, he lunged swiftly and sliced one wing off. Desperate now, Jatayu hit him on his face with the other wing, flapping it around like a giant windmill and knocking Ravana's crowns off. He swooped down and clawed Ravana's arms, gouging them with his sharp talons. But Ravana grew twenty more arms to fight him.

The air around the chariot grew dense with flying feathers and blood, but the king of demons and the old bird fought on. The mules kicked and rose and fell, and Sita hid her face in her hands. She could not bear to see the old bird's struggles, and called Rama's name over and over again, almost without being aware of what she was saying.

With one great blow, Ravana cut off Jatayu's remaining wing. The valiant warrior hurtled from the skies, still murmuring, 'I must save Sita, I must save her.' His eyes were blind with blood and his body covered with wounds. As he fell, he could only hear Sita's voice, though it was a despairing whisper from the chariot. 'O Jatayu, noble king, thank you! You have fought so bravely for me. Please tell my husband what happened, please tell Rama…'

Sita leaned over the side of the chariot, watching Jatayu's form spin out of sight to the ground. She dropped the flowers in her hair and watched them drift to the ground, hoping Rama would find them and recognize them. An immense sadness filled her heart. After a while, her eyes fell on the thin gold bangles she wore. She took off her bangles and threw them down as well. Then she leaned over and thought that she, too, should jump out.

But Ravana pulled her back roughly with one arm, while the other whipped the mules to make them fly faster and faster. The golden chariot sped like an arrow of fire heading in the direction of the sea.

The gods in heaven looked down and saw Sita crying, but they could not do anything to help her. Ravana was too powerful for them. Only Rama could save her, but first he would have to fight a long and fierce battle with Ravana. This was the reason he had been born on earth, and the time to fight his greatest enemy was upon him.

The Search for Sita

'Sita, Sita,' called Rama, running through the forest towards the hut. Running towards him from that direction was his brother, who looked distraught. He knew then that something was very wrong, for otherwise Lakshmana would have never left Sita alone.

'Sita? Where is she?' he asked urgently.

'We heard you cry out…' replied Lakshmana, and the two brothers did not speak any more, but ran as fast as they could towards the hut.

The clearing and the hut were strangely quiet. There were no birds or animals anywhere. A broken leaf-plate, berries and jasmines were scattered on the ground. The circle Lakshmana had drawn smouldered in a line of dying fire. They rushed into the hut, and out again, all around the clearing, and on their usual forest paths. But of Sita there was no sign.

'Something terrible has happened to her. I know it. O Lakshmana, why did you leave her?' said Rama sorrowfully, and would not let his brother explain how he had been forced to go and look for him.

Overcome with sorrow, Rama wandered around the clearing and went up to every tree that Sita loved. He ran weeping into the forest, looking for signs of her. 'Sita, Sita,' he wept. Then he turned to Lakshmana, his eyes red with grief. 'The sun knows where Sita is, but it will not tell me. The winds blow everywhere, they must know, but they, too, do not speak to me. O Lakshmana, I shall go mad with grief if I do not find Sita.' And the great hero wept as if he were a child, holding the jasmine buds that Sita had picked early that morning, which now seemed so far away.

Lakshmana, feeling helpless, suddenly noticed that the deer, which had moved away when the golden deer appeared, had come back into the clearing, and a group of them wandered very close to where the brothers sat, as if trying to tell them something. 'Look, Rama, see how the deer lift their heads to the sky and then turn their heads to the south. They want to show us something.'

Rama got up quickly and they walked in the direction the deer seemed to be indicating. After a while, they came to clearing in the forest where some crushed flowers were strewn on the ground. 'These are the flowers Sita was wearing in her hair. I gave them to her this morning,' Rama said, picking up the torn petals and holding them close to his heart.

They walked on further until Lakshmana suddenly exclaimed. He had spotted something in nearby bushes. He went closer and cleared away the big leaves to look more closely. It was a broken chariot wheel. His hands felt sticky and he looked down, startled to see that they were red with blood. 'Rama, come here!' he called out. 'Look, a chariot wheel—it seems to be made of gold, with jewels.'

Rama ran over. They looked at the wheel and wondered what it meant. Then, beside the trunk of a long-dead tree they saw a clump of feathers, torn and covered in blood.

'That looks like part of a giant bird's wing. What could have happened here? Did this demon carry Sita away, or...' Lakshmana stopped, unable to put into words the image in his mind—Sita eaten up or mauled by a ferocious demon.

When Rama looked at the blood on the ground, he understood what Lakshmana had not been able to say. His gentle face became flushed with fury and his eyes gleamed in a dark line of rage. 'I will kill any demon who has touched a hair on my Sita's head,' he said through lips that trembled with anger. His quiet voice echoed through the trees. 'I will destroy all creation if my Sita is not returned to me—the gods in heaven, the demons in hell, all will pay. With this bow I will burn up the waters of every river and ocean; I will empty the three worlds of all beings; I will dislodge the sun and the moon from the sky. You will see, Lakshmana, as I burn this universe with my wrath.'

As Rama reached his hand to pull an arrow out from the quiver, Lakshmana, who had never seen his brother in such a rage, quickly went to him and touched his arm. 'Rama, do not speak thus. You are the most kind and noble of all men, who cannot harm an insect unless there is dire necessity. How can you speak of destroying the universe? Calm yourself, my lord. Remember who you are. Remember what you have always told me: anger overpowers reason and justice. How can you punish the innocent for the misdeeds of one demon? You must seek out the one who has wronged you and punish him with your mighty powers.'

As Rama listened, his anger melted away. He lowered his bow and sighed deeply. 'You are right, my brother. I am so filled with sorrow that I cannot think properly. Tell me what we should do now. How should we find Sita?'

Lakshmana got up quickly. He knew it was time to act. 'Come, let us search this place for more signs. Look, there are some more feathers and something else...' He ran further south into the forest, pointing at the fragments on the ground that his sharp eyes had spotted.

Rama followed more slowly, thinking of Sita and how she would have looked at the new trees and flowers with joy. Tears welled up in his eyes.

Lakshmana's sudden shout startled him. 'Look at that, Rama!' He was pointing to a huge pile of feathers that lay on the ground some distance away and could barely be seen through the thick bushes. The two brothers ran swiftly in that direction, Lakshmana raising his bow and arrow in case it was a demon waiting for them. Then, as Rama came up, there was a cry of pain and both of them recognized Jatayu's voice.

The old bird was dying, his breath slowly ebbing away. He was still alive only because he had willed himself to live until he could talk to Rama. 'Come near, my lord, I have not much time to live,' he whispered painfully. 'I tried to save Sita, but I could not. Ravana, the king of Lanka, carried her away in his chariot ... I fought with him, but could not stop him ... He cut my wings off. Save her, my lord, make haste! Only you can save her ...' With one last painful gasp, the breath left Jatayu's body.

A deep sorrow filled Rama and Lakshmana. 'O great king of birds, may you live forever in heaven,' said Rama as he stroked Jatayu's head. 'You gave your life to save Sita, just as you said you would.'

They gave the bird a loving funeral, reciting prayers on the banks of the river as the sun set. Jatayu's soul rose into the sky and found a place in heaven with other kind and noble beings.

Kabandha

Rama and Lakshmana walked on without knowing where they were going. They walked in silence, each thinking of the sad things that had happened in the last few hours, as darkness fell.

The forest grew darker as they walked and giant trees blocked their way. Rocks grew out of the ground like pillars and strange animals called from the black caves.

Suddenly, they heard a terrible noise as if all the trees in the forest were crashing on the ground. Tigers began to roar and wild elephants came stomping towards them, trumpeting violently as if they had gone mad.

Lakshmana looked up to see what was causing this noise and then he saw the demon. It was the weirdest monster he had ever seen. It was as tall as a mountain, but it had no head. Its mouth was set in its enormous hairy stomach. It had one huge blinking eye which was right in the middle of its chest, and this eye was now staring at them crookedly.

The mouth in the stomach spoke in a gurgling way. 'Come, my dear ones, let me eat you up… My name is Kabandha and I love human flesh. I do not care what your names are since soon you will be food for my stomach… Urhhhhh!' moaned the mouth joyfully.

It reached down with its very long arms. Rama and Lakshmana turned to run but the demon's arms twisted and wound their way over and under the trees like a pair of giant pythons, swooping with incredible speed. Each giant hand seized one of the princes firmly, and snaked back to the body. Then the monster began to move them rapidly up and down, between its giant eye and its foul-smelling, drooling mouth. They could see its teeth, blackened and covered with rotting bits of flesh, but as sharp as razors. As it spoke, the drool flew and fell all over them like sticky rain. 'Aha! What joy to have caught two little fellows in one swoop. Now sit quietly, my dear ones. Stay quiet. I like to chew the arms and legs first, then the body, and the heads last of all.'

Rama and Lakshmana were dazed from being tossed around so close to the demon's putrid mouth. Yet they struggled madly, trying to twist around in the huge fists to reach their weapons.

'Frisky, eh?' the monster frowned. 'Let me quieten you down... a few tosses should do it!' And it began to swing them up and down violently until they were dizzy.

'Rama, we have to kill this demon! I'll strike and distract it, and you escape!' shouted Lakshmana. He tried to keep his balance, but the demon was twirling him above its body.

'Lakshmana, we will strike both its arms together. You shoot your arrow the very moment I let mine loose,' gasped Rama.

'Enough of playing!' wheezed the stomach-mouth. 'Now, let me think. Shall I eat you together or you first or you? Difficult to decide... Aghhhaa.' The giant eye shut as the monster thought.

'Now,' signalled Rama, and before the demon could open its eye, Rama and Lakshmana reached for their bows and sent two arrows flying from either side. The arrows hit where the monster's arms joined its shoulders and sliced off its arms. They then turned and pierced its stomach on either side of the mouth, flew through the body and returned to the quiver, shining clean.

The demon's grip loosened and Rama and Lakshmana leapt out, just as it fell to the ground with a deafening growl, blood flowing from its stomach-mouth. The weight of its mammoth body shook the earth, and made lakes flood and nearby hills crack open wide. All the fierce forest creatures—tigers, crocodiles and elephants—shut their eyes in fear. The smaller animals ran and hid inside nearby caves.

As soon as Kabandha hit the ground, the armless torso twitching furiously, the bleeding mouth spoke again. But the voice had changed completely. 'I was waiting for this day for countless years,' it said in a gentle voice. 'You are Rama and you have come here to save me. I thank you. Your golden arrow has set me free from Indra's curse.' It was breathing heavily now, the words coming in gasps. 'Once I was as handsome as the moon and lived in heaven. But I was very naughty. I would change into an ugly demon to amuse myself and frighten everyone. The holy men and Indra cursed me, and I became the demon I used to pretend to be. When they saw me, they felt sorry for me and said, "Wait in this forest. One day Rama will come this way and set you free." Put this monstrous body of mine in the fire when I die, I beg of you.' And saying this, Kabandha died.

Rama and Lakshmana did as Kabandha asked. As soon as the flames touched the ugly form, a beautiful creature rose from it. He raised his hands to the sky and a golden chariot appeared, drawn by six white horses. He got into it.

The heavenly creature turned to Rama. 'Go to Pampa Lake, beyond those hills you see on the horizon. There, in the forest where all the trees and flowers of heaven bloom, you will meet Sugriva, the chief of the monkeys. He will help you get your wife back.' And with these words, the chariot flew up and disappeared among the high clouds.

The Monkey Clans

Early the following morning, Rama and Lakshmana began walking towards the hills.

The path climbed and meandered through a line of fragrant flowering trees. The forest was lit by soft silver-gold light, as if it were twilight all the time. Hundreds of blue and green birds sang as they flew around the trees. As they walked, they saw giant fruits in strange shapes and huge drifts of flowers in blue, gold and green. Enormous butterflies hovered around their heads. Some had purple wings with blue dots, while others were pure white, like pieces of shining silver. A herd of elephants came out to look at them, waving a friendly greeting with their trunks. But the two brothers were too anxious to enjoy the sights.

At last, they crossed the hills and came to a lake surrounded by trees. It glistened in the silver light like a huge oval sapphire and swans glided on its surface. Hundreds of pink lotuses bloomed everywhere. 'This must be Pampa Lake,' said Lakshmana.

As they stood in the shade of a kadamba tree, a hundred monkeys watched them from hidden hideouts in the forest. 'Who are they?' 'What are they doing in our forest?' they chattered to one another in low voices. 'They look like princes, brave and proud.' 'Yet they walk barefeet!' 'They carry bows and arrows.' 'But they wear bark and have matted hair like hermits.' 'Have they come to attack us?' All this excited chatter travelled through the trees faster than the monkeys could go, and finally reached the ears of their chief, Sugriva, who was sitting in his cave deep in the forest.

'Is it someone Vaali has sent?' Sugriva asked anxiously. 'Someone go find out who the strangers are.'

'If you allow me, I shall go and see what they want,' said Hanuman, the bravest and cleverest in the monkey clan.

From the time he was born, Hanuman's mother knew that he was an extraordinary monkey with special powers. His father was Vayu, the god of wind, and his mother was a beautiful heavenly creature who had come to live on earth for a while. When he was a baby, Hanuman once flew right up to the sun and grabbed hold of it. 'What a pretty red fruit,' he said admiringly. He did not notice that around him the earth was plunged into darkness and all creatures were frantic with worry.

Finally, Indra, to protect the sun, threw his thunderbolt at Hanuman. Enraged at this attack on his son, Vayu stopped all the winds from blowing. All living creatures on earth started to die for there was no air to breathe. Only when the gods promised to give Hanuman many boons did Vayu allow the winds to move again. As a result of these boons, Hanuman could change his shape, fly anywhere and defeat even the mightiest in battle. Despite his great strength, however, Hanuman was not proud.

He was kind to all the monkeys who were not as strong or clever as he, and very loyal to his chief, Sugriva.

Hanuman jumped over the trees and headed for the place where Rama and Lakshmana were standing. On the way, he changed himself into a human so that the strangers would not be bewildered by a talking monkey. When he reached Rama and Lakshmana, he looked like an old man.

'Greetings, strangers,' he said in a gentle voice. 'May I ask who you are and what brings you to this remote forest?' As he said these words, he experienced a strange sensation within himself. It felt as if a wave of pure happiness and love flooded every bit of his body. He bowed his head and spoke again, 'You are princes; that I can tell from your noble bearing. Yet you are dressed like holy men. Are you looking for someone? Can I help you?'

Rama looked at him and he, too, felt some ancient bond with the small man standing in front of him. He smiled gently at him, wondering who he was.

Hanuman could no longer keep up the pretence. 'My lord,' he said reverently, 'your presence makes my heart fill with joy. I am Hanuman. I am a monkey but I can change into any form. I have come here because my chief, Sugriva, wished to know what you were doing here. Sugriva was driven out of his kingdom by his brother, Vaali. And he thinks you might have been sent by Vaali to kill him. But I do not think that can be true, for I see nothing but goodness in you.' He transformed himself into his original form as he spoke.

Rama reached out and patted him, and spoke in a gentle voice. 'It is very fortunate that you have come to us, Hanuman. We are looking for your chief, Sugriva. We need his help to find my wife, Sita, who has been kidnapped by the king of demons.'

Hanuman rose quickly and made himself as huge as a hill. 'Please sit on my shoulders and I will carry both of you to my chief,' he said. When they were seated, he flew like the wind over the treetops and reached the secret clearing surrounded by caves where Sugriva was waiting.

The monkeys began running around in a frenzy when they saw Hanuman land with Rama and Lakshmana on his shoulders. 'Do not fear them,' said Hanuman quickly and loudly. 'They are not from Vaali. They are good humans, noble princes of royal blood. They need our help.'

The monkeys calmed down and began to gather around in a friendly manner. Many more came out of hiding and greeted Rama and Lakshmana. Finally, Sugriva came out to greet them and they all sat down together in the shade of a banyan tree. Young monkeys were sent off to fetch cool water and pluck fresh fruits from the trees for the two brothers.

Rama asked Sugriva why he was so terrified of Vaali. Sugriva sighed and began telling them the sad story of his life.

'Vaali and I were once devoted to each other. He was the elder one and ruled over our father's kingdom, Kishkinda. I was happy to serve him as a younger brother should.

'One stormy night, a rakshasa came to the palace gates and challenged Vaali to a fight. Vaali was always extremely proud of his strength and could never refuse a challenge so he rushed out to fight the rakshasa. I, too, followed, but when the rakshasa saw both of us, he ran away into the forest. Vaali and I chased him, but he went and hid inside a deep cave.

'"You wait outside. Do not come in," said Vaali to me. "I will go and kill that demon. If you see milk flowing out, you will know that I have won, but if you see blood flowing out, you will know that I am dead. You must then go back to Kishkinda and rule in my place." And then he disappeared into the dark cave.

'I waited outside for many months, but Vaali did not come out. I heard terrible sounds, screams and wails from inside the cave, but I did not go in for he had forbidden me. Then, one day, blood began to flow out. I was very frightened. I thought the rakshasa had killed my brother, and would now come out to get me. I wanted to fight my brother's killer, but I remembered what Vaali had told me. So I quickly blocked the mouth of the cave with large boulders and went back.

'I came back to the palace, very grieved at having lost my dear brother. Our kingdom had lost its king. In all these months, there had been no one to govern and enemies had begun to threaten it. The ministers insisted that I become king. I agreed, for the sake of Kishkinda's security and also because Vaali had also asked me to do so.

'After many months, Vaali suddenly returned one day. He was covered with wounds, and his rage was terrible to see. "You left me to die, you traitor. I will kill you," he screamed at me. I tried again and again to explain what had happened but he would not listen. He began to beat me up and shouted, "Out, you rat, out of my sight before I strangle you with my bare hands."

'I wanted to say how sorry I was and he could have his throne back. I wanted to say that I was very happy to serve him as a loyal subject. But he would not listen to me and threw me out of the palace. I lost my home, my family, and now I have to hide here in this forest like a wild beast. Vaali cannot come here because there is a curse. Otherwise, he would have killed me by now,' said Sugriva sadly. 'I really did not want his kingdom. I would never have left him in the cave if I had thought he was still alive.'

After a moment, Rama spoke. 'I can feel your sorrow. I have lost my father, my kingdom and now my beloved wife. We must be brave and help each other.'

Sugriva looked up at Rama. 'I would be so grateful if you could help me regain my home and my family, and defeat my brother who is out to kill me. Maybe I, too, can be of some help to you. You have heard my story, now tell me yours.'

Lakshmana explained why they were in the forest, and told Sugriva all that had happened from the time that they were banished until Sita was taken away. 'While looking for her, we met a demon who turned out to be a heavenly being.

He told us that you would be able to help us to find Sita, which is why we came in search of you.'

Hanuman, who was listening quietly, suddenly jumped up. 'We saw her! We saw the demon-king flying through the clouds in a golden chariot when we were sitting on top of that hill yesterday. At first we thought it was a thunderbolt hurtling across the sky, then we saw there were people in the chariot: the demon-king and a woman. She was leaning over the side and she threw something down. We picked it up. Wait, I will get it for you.'

From a nearby cave, Hanuman fetched a bundle of yellow cloth, such as the monkeys wore. Rama opened the bundle. In it was a pair of gold bangles. He reached forward and picked them up. He looked at them and then held them against his cheek. 'Yes, yes, these are hers. These were the only ornaments she wore when we left the palace,' he whispered and turned away to hide his tears.

Hanuman's heart was filled with sadness when he saw Rama's unhappy face. He jumped up and spoke, 'I will find Sita for you, my lord, whatever happens. Command me and I shall do whatever you desire.'

Rama rose and embraced him. The monkey spoke with such warmth and affection that he and Lakshmana felt that he had been their friend all their lives, and perhaps even before.

They sat together on a rock and talked late into the night, sharing their hopes and fears, joys and sorrows. Owls hooted far away and fireflies danced around their heads. One by one, hundreds of stars peeped out in the sky to watch them.

When dawn came, Hanuman lit a fire with sandalwood logs and gathered some flowers from the shrubs nearby. He, Rama, Lakshmana and Sugriva prayed to the fire god and offered him flowers, asking him to forge their friendship. The sun rose as they prayed and a gentle breeze blew, making a shower of white champa blossoms fall around them in a circle.

'That is a good omen,' said Rama. 'The trees are blessing our friendship. From now on, we will share everything, whether it is happiness or sorrow, wealth or poverty.'

Rama and Lakshmana decided that first they would help Sugriva in his fight against Vaali. They sat and planned how they could do this. 'You challenge him to a battle and Rama will slay him,' suggested Lakshmana.

Sugriva was silent for a while and then spoke. 'My brother is one of the most ferocious warriors on earth. Let me tell you a tale about his immense strength. There was once a demon named Dhundubhi, who was as strong as a thousand elephants. This demon was very fond of changing his shape; he especially liked being a buffalo that could fly as swiftly as an eagle. Dhundubhi loved fighting, but as he was so powerful, no one wanted to take him on.

'One day, bored with having no one to fight, he flew to the sea and threw a challenge to Varuna, the god of the seas. "Come and fight with me or I will drink up all your water," he yelled above the crashing waves. The lord of seas was in no mood to fight this mad demon, so he replied, "O Dhundubhi, you are too mighty for me to fight. Go to the lord of the mountains. He is tall and hefty, his body is full of rocks. He would be a better opponent."

'Dhundubhi flew to the mountains. There, high on a snowy peak, he saw Himavat, the god of the mountains, swirling around like a huge cloud. "Come and fight with me or I will trample your forests and crush your rocky hills," he yelled. Himavat looked down and smiled at him gently. "We know how strong you are, and we do not want to fight with you. We live here peacefully and do not know the art of war. You need a more worthy opponent—someone you can wrestle with and try out all kinds of new tricks on. Go to Kishkinda. There you will find the king of monkeys, Vaali. He is as strong as you are, if not stronger. He never refuses to fight and he can give you the best battle you have ever had."

'Dhundubhi, thrilled to have at last found a good fighter, flew at top speed to Kishkinda, singing all the way. People looking up at the sky were amazed to see a huge black buffalo bellowing loudly and clapping his front hooves with joy as he flew.

'When he arrived at the gates of Vaali's palace, Dhundubhi grew to twice his old size. Pawing the ground with his great hooves and snorting fire through his nostrils, he called out to Vaali, "Come and fight, O Vaali."

'Vaali was with his queen when he heard this roar below his window. He leaned out and saw the buffalo. Annoyed, he yelled back, "Go away, you stupid beast. If you want to stay alive, get out from my city."

'But Dhundubhi would not move. He kept bellowing, "Come and fight. The god of the mountains said you love a good fight, but I find that you are a coward, a weakling who likes to laze all day in the women's palace, eating sweets and drinking wine."

'Vaali jumped up with rage when he heard this. "Wait, you idiotic buffalo. I will behead you with my bare hands," he shouted and jumped out of the window. He landed right on the buffalo-demon's back and they began to fight.

'Both were equally powerful and they fought all day long. All around them, people, monkeys and gods watched. Finally, Vaali lifted the demon, swirled him around and then flung him on the ground so hard that Dhundubhi died at once. Even then, Vaali was not happy. He picked up the huge carcass as if it were a pebble and flung him far away to the forest. When the buffalo-demon's body was flying through the sky, drops of blood fell on a hermit's ashram. He cursed Vaali and that is why he can never enter this forest.' Sugriva pointed at a hillock in the distance. 'Look, there lies the huge carcass of Dhundubhi, which was flung from Kishkinda to this place by my brother. See, that is how strong he is.'

Lakshmana laughed when he saw the monkey-chief looking so worried. 'Your brother may be strong, but my brother is the greatest warrior on earth. His arrows are like the rays of the sun. They go everywhere in a fleeting moment, yet none can touch them.' He turned to Rama and asked him to send an arrow into a sal tree that stood on the horizon.

Rama smiled and pulled a single gold-tipped arrow from his quiver. He bent the bow and, pulling the string close to his ear, sent the arrow flying. Flying more swiftly than the eye could see, the arrow pierced the sal tree and then the six trees standing behind it. It then turned around and returned to the quiver.

The monkeys were awed into silence. 'Do not ever doubt my brother,' said Lakshmana. 'A single arrow will be enough to kill an army. Vaali is only one monkey. Challenge him to a fight, and Rama will help you finish him off.'

Kishkinda

They set off at once for Kishkinda. When they reached the city, Rama and Lakshmana stayed hidden behind a tree while Sugriva went to the palace.

He went boldly up to the gates and began shouting, 'Vaali, come out and fight. This is Sugriva and I have come to take revenge on you because you threw me out of my home unjustly.'

At first, Vaali could not believe his ears. 'Has my stupid brother lost his mind? How dare he come back! I will put an end to his miserable life,' he shouted and rushed out.

The two brothers began to fight. Dust rose in the air like a cloud; there were grunts and yells and thuds, and blood splashed all over. Though Rama wanted to help Sugriva, he could not identify him in the tangle of limbs. Both brothers fought in the same way and looked alike. Finally, as night fell, the battle was called off for the day. Sugriva was bruised and bloodied, but he was proud to have survived.

The next day, Rama made Sugriva wear a garland of flowers around his neck. Sugriva was in poor condition after a night of pain. They set off again for the palace gates and soon the battle resumed. Vaali began to wrestle with his brother, and it was obvious that today he was stronger than Sugriva. Rama waited anxiously, his bow at the ready.

Just as Vaali was about to strangle Sugriva with his powerful grip, Rama sent an arrow flying towards them. The arrow, flying straight and true, whizzed through the dust and pierced Vaali's throat. Vaali fell down at once, dead.

Rama was unhappy to have shot a warrior while he was battling another, but he had promised to help Sugriva as that was the only way to get Sita back.

There was confusion and chaos in Kishkinda when the monkey clan heard that their king had died. But Rama soon restored order and installed Sugriva as the king. Vaali's son, Angad, was made the yuvraj, and gradually peace and order returned to the kingdom.

The rainy season now began, and Rama and Lakshmana had to discontinue their search for Sita.

While Sugriva ruled from the palace, Hanuman waited with the princes in a cave in the forest because he knew how sad and weary these days were for them. Dark clouds covered the sky, and there was no daylight for days. Torrents of rain flooded the forest paths, making their cave damp and musty. Snakes crawled out of their pits and hung about the mouth of the cave. Food became scarce and harder to find. Rama grew sadder with each passing day for there was no news of Sita.

The Search Begins

At last the rains stopped and the sky was clear once more. The air was sweet with the scent of freshly washed leaves, and new flowers bloomed everywhere.

Hanuman was waiting for this day and he ran to the palace to remind Sugriva of his promise to help find Sita. The monkey-chief had not forgotten his pledge and ordered his commander-in-chief to get the army ready. 'All corners of the earth must be searched till Sita is found. Send word that all the monkeys and our allies, the bears, have to join in this search at once,' Sugriva declared in court.

The message was sent across the kingdom, and soon the monkeys and the bears began to pour into Kishkinda. Monkeys of every race and breed came marching in from the forests, coasts and mountains. Some of the monkeys were tall and lanky with silver coats, some were muscular and black with pink noses, while others were short and stocky with cheeky red faces. Many of the bears had grizzly coats as they had come down from the high Himalayas and they sweated profusely in the heat of Kishkinda.

As thousands of monkeys and bears gathered at the palace gates, Sugriva said to Rama, 'This vast army of mine is now yours. They are waiting for your orders. At your command, they will set out in all eight directions to search for Sita.'

Rama thanked Sugriva and addressed the assembled army. He described how Sita had been abducted by the demon-king and had last been seen flying through the sky in his chariot. He did now know for sure where Ravana had taken her, though he suspected it was to his kingdom of Lanka, which lay to the far south. Rama asked the army to find her.

The eight generals met for a conference to map out their routes and decide the area each would cover with his unit. All of them were asked to come back to Kishkinda in two months' time to report what they had found. Though Lanka was the most obvious place to seek her, they needed to look everywhere in case Ravana had hidden her away in the territory of one of the kings he had conquered.

'But what about Lanka? How can we find Sita if Ravana has crossed the seas with her? We have no navy,' said one general in a worried voice.

'I will find a way to get there and look for her,' said Hanuman.

Rama was overjoyed. 'Take this ring of mine and tell her you are my most valued messenger. Hanuman, I know in my heart you will bring Sita back to me,' he said.

With much fanfare, the army marched out of the city the following morning and headed in different directions. Their families lined the roads as they marched out, and many baby monkeys wept at the thought of not being able to see their fathers for two long months.

'But how do I get to Lanka?' Hanuman wondered, as he set off with one of the generals going south. This continued to worry him over the following days and weeks as the army marched southwards.

They passed through strange forests, some full of blue light, others as dark as the night even during the day. Some had trees without any leaves, while others were so dense with foliage that they had to hack a way through. They saw ancient rivers, which were now filled with lava, and rocks carved into strange shapes by ice. Everywhere they went, they asked everyone they met whether they had seen Sita, but no one had.

Then, after many weeks, they came to a forest where there was nothing but sand and the ghostly trunks of dead trees rising straight and thin like pillars. This forest seemed never-ending, and as they walked on hour after hour, the monkeys became more and more hungry and thirsty. After half a day of this, many did not have the strength to go on and started fainting on the dry sand.

As they were losing hope, Hanuman saw a flock of waterbirds flying out of a cave in the distance. 'Look, their beaks are wet!' he cried out. 'There must be some water there. Come, let us go in.'

He led the way into the cave, which was cool and green. Creepers hung over the rocks, and it was so dark that the monkeys had to hold hands and walk in a line. They were a little scared, but their thirst pushed them ahead. Suddenly, a glittering light blinded Hanuman and the others in front. 'What is this?' gasped the general, covering his eyes.

The monkeys stopped and stared. The cave was so large that it seemed to be another world, as large as the one outside. It was filled with trees that shone like gold. As they went nearer, they could see that the leaves were made of gold and the fruits of silver. A pond with clear water gleamed with gems of all hues, and the air was fragrant with flowers. All around the pond were the most wonderful fruit trees, full of ripe fruit. Each tree had many kinds of fruit—apples, bananas, peaches and pears. In the distance, against a pink sky, there were sliver mansions glittering like large stars.

The monkeys were so enchanted by all the beautiful things around them that they forgot their thirst, though they had finally found water. 'Where are we?' they whispered. 'Is this real?'

Just then a woman came out of the mansion nearest to them. She looked at them sadly. 'Why are you here?' she asked in a sweet, clear voice. 'Your greed has led you to your doom. This is the magical garden created by the demon-magician Maya. Those who enter here can never return.'

The monkeys were shocked out of their amazement. Some of the younger ones began to cry. Even the old general looked sad. Hanuman asked the woman, 'Is there no way out? We did not come to steal the treasures, we came in because we were thirsty and there seemed to be water here.'

The woman looked closely into his eyes and suddenly smiled. 'You are a good-hearted monkey and I will help you,' she said. 'Drink this cool water and have some fruit to eat. Then close your eyes and do not open them till I ask you to.'

The monkeys quickly drank some water, but no one felt like eating the fruit, delicious though it looked. Hanuman, however, ate a big bunch of bananas with relish. Then they all shut their eyes and waited.

The woman clapped her hands twice and all the monkeys could feel the air around them change. When they opened their eyes, they found themselves in a green forest from where they could see something very blue in the distance. They had reached the ocean!

'I never thought I would get away,' said a young monkey to his fellow soldier, wiping the sweat from his forehead. 'I never thought I would get to see the sea!' In their relief and excitement, the young monkeys frolicked by the water, chattering amongst themselves.

The general, Hanuman and other senior officers, however, were worried. They gathered together on some rocks and discussed the situation.

'Now what shall we do? We still have no word of Sita!' said the general. 'We have already spent six weeks on the road. Our king said we must return within two months! We do not have time to find a boat and sail to Lanka to look for her. Besides, that would be very dangerous.'

'I will fly there and look for her,' said Hanuman.

'No, no, it is too dangerous. You have never flown such a great distance, and over the sea, too. If you fall, you will drown,' said the general.

'Besides, there is nothing to show she is there. Jatayu told Rama that Sita was taken south. But we have seen no sign. Could Ravana have turned his chariot north again?' asked an officer with large whiskers.

'I know it is dangerous, but I promised Rama I would deliver his ring to her. What other way is there but to go myself and see?' asked Hanuman. There was a moment of silence as they all thought hard.

Suddenly a voice called out, making the monkeys jump in surprise. 'O monkeys, are you talking about my brother Jatayu? Is he well?'

The voice seemed to be coming from the branch of a dead tree nearby. Looking closer, the monkeys realized that the branch was actually an ancient eagle, perhaps the oldest creature they had ever seen. He was dark and shrivelled like wood, and instead of the magnificent wings of his kind, he had two broken stumps.

It was Sampati, Jatayu's bother, who had saved him from being burnt by the sun. He had spent many years seeking news of his brother, but as he could not fly, he could only ask those who came to him. Now finally he heard someone speak the name he longed to hear. 'Jatayu—my brother Jatayu? Are these monkeys talking about my brother?' he wondered.

Sampati moved closer to them and croaked again, 'You know my brother, Jatayu?'

Once he recovered from his surprise, Hanuman did not want to tell the old eagle the sad news, but he had to. 'Your brother is dead,' he said gently. 'But he died like a true hero…' and he told Sampati the whole story. 'And that is why we are here,' he ended. 'We are trying to find where Ravana has hidden Sita. We think he might have taken her to Lanka, but we do not know how to find out.'

Sampati had shut his old eyes when he heard about his brother's death, but now he opened them and looked sharply at Hanuman. 'If Ravana has killed my brother, then I will help you find Ravana so that he, too, can be killed. Because I cannot fly, over the years my eyes have learnt to see very far. My eyes are old now, but I can still see much further than any of you. Wait here! I will hop to that high rock and look as hard as I can at Lanka and I will tell you what I can see.' And with that Sampati rose tiredly. With odd jerks he hopped from rock to rock, until he reached the highest one that looked out to the sea.

A while passed, and then suddenly Sampati turned. There was something different about him, and they realized what it was when he suddenly spread out magnificent wings and soared back to where the monkeys were waiting.

'I have seen her,' he said, as soon as he reached them. 'It must have been her, for the gods have blessed me and my wings have grown again.' He spread them out as if he could not believe it. 'I saw the great golden city, and in a garden I saw a beautiful woman crying. She was more beautiful than any other woman I have ever seen. There was a circle of demonesses sitting around her.'

Hanuman jumped up with joy. 'I know now for certain she is there! I will go at once, taking Rama's ring,' he said.

Hanuman in Lanka

Hanuman did not waste any time. He took a deep breath and his body began to grow. Soon he was enormous, as tall as a hill, with a tail as long as a giant serpent. Pressing his foot against a rocky hill and folding his ears back, he took a flying leap and rose high into the sky. All the other monkeys watched him, breathless with wonder, and then moved back as the trees on the shore began to shake.

Hanuman flew at great speed, his arms outstretched, his tail floating behind him. The winds roared with joy for he was their prince, the son of the wind god, and blew at him to help his flight. Hanuman soared, playing hide-and-seek with the clouds. The force of the wind made the waves toss up, and dolphins, whales, sea lions and fishes peered out of the sea to see this flying wonder.

A mountain rose to block his way, but Hanuman struck it with his chest. The mountain bent low quickly, 'I am sorry, my son. I did not want to get in your way. Stop and rest on me for a while. I thought you were one of us. Once all mountains had wings and could fly, but Indra clipped our wings. Your father, Vayu, saved me and now I hide in this sea,' it said with a mighty rumble.

'I am sorry to have hurt you, but I am in a great hurry,' shouted Hanuman, rushing past.

But he could not go far, for behind the mountain lurked an enormous sea monster. 'Stop,' she screeched. 'None can pass this way without going through my mouth.'

Hanuman did not want to waste time arguing with the monster. He quickly made himself even larger. As he grew, the sea monster opened her mouth wider and wider to swallow him.

Suddenly, Hanuman made himself into a tiny creature, no bigger than a bee. Before the monster could notice, he flew right into her mouth and then flew out again swiftly. 'Now let me pass,' he laughed.

The sea monster smiled back at him and lowered her face. 'That was clever,' she said. 'I am the queen of the serpents. You have my blessings now. Go and be successful.'

Hanuman flew on happily but then just as he was picking up speed, something pulled him back. He looked all around him but could not see anything that could be dragging him down. Finally, he looked below at the sea. There swam a huge demoness. She was holding on to the shadow of his tail, which fell on the water. Hanuman, annoyed that his flight was being interrupted so frequently, swooped down, freed his shadow and ripped her stomach apart. Then he flew on again.

The sun was like a pink ball of fire. Clouds rushed past and the winds carried him over the sea. Suddenly, as Hanuman looked down, there were no more rolling waves but the green island of Lanka below him.

'How will I find Sita on this huge island? Sampati said she was in a garden, but there must be many gardens,' thought Hanuman, as he made himself his usual size again and prepared to land. He flew up to the gates of the city and then hid himself behind a tree while he thought of a plan.

'The best plan is to wait for the night. Then I will make myself smaller and sneak into the palace grounds. Ravana must have kept Sita prisoner in some garden there,' he decided.

He waited until evening fell and the city was lit with lamps. The streets, paved with gems, began to shine, and tall mansions glittered as one by one lamps were lit in their golden rooms. The magnificent city perched on a hilltop began to shimmer. It looked as if it was floating in air.

'How beautiful this city is! But it is full of fierce demons, all armed and ready to attack,' thought Hanuman. 'First, I must find Sita, then maybe I can have some fun with a few of these demons.'

He made himself as small as a kitten, and slithered over the city walls and found the palace without too much difficulty. He hid behind a bush and looked around carefully. There were two guards, huge demons, walking back and forth in front of the gates.

He dashed towards the gates when the guards were not looking. One of the guards caught a glimpse of something and asked the other, 'Did you see that little monkey?'

'No,' growled the other. 'You must be dreaming. Wake up or else I will clobber you with my club.'

Hanuman smiled to himself. He crept up behind the second guard and tweaked his hair. As he looked around, Hanuman sneaked in through the gate. Behind him, he could hear yells of rage. 'How dare you pull my hair,' shouted the second guard, hitting the other guard with his club. 'I did not... the monkey...' said the guard, rolled his eyes and fainted.

Hanuman ran swiftly along the huge driveway and slipped in through a side door. He found himself right inside Ravana's gorgeous palace. The gold and silver dazzled his eyes as he walked around searching for Sita. Demon-guards marched up and down, but Hanuman was so small and he hid himself so well that no one noticed him. As he slunk through the corridors, he saw beautiful women dozing on sandalwood beds. They were dressed in robes of silk which were embroidered with diamonds, pearls and rubies. Musicians played softly, and fountains sprinkled cool scented water. In a banquet room, elderly demons chomped hungrily on whole legs of sheep and camels.

'Where is Sita? She cannot be one of these women, I know. I do not know what she looks like, but my heart will know when I see her,' thought Hanuman. He kept trying to find a way out to the garden, but each room led only to another more splendid one, and he could see no sign of gardens.

Finally, after walking through about a hundred rooms, he peeped out of a small window and there outside was a lovely garden, gleaming in the moonlight. Big green trees swayed in the soothing breeze and their leaves shone as if covered with silver dust. Huge flowers bloomed everywhere and their sweet scent made Hanuman dizzy as he slipped out of the window and made his way out. Stepping carefully on the soft white sand, he made his way towards a pond, where little goldfish played among the lotuses. Hanuman looked around in wonder.

Then he saw her. She was sitting silently, her sad face pale and thin in the bright moonlight. A circle of demonesses sat around her, exactly as Sampati had described.

Hanuman swung through the trees, until he was near her. As if she knew he was hidden there, Sita turned her face towards him. Hanuman gasped when he saw her beautiful eyes full of tears. 'This is Sita, I know. How exquisite and fragile she is! I must find a way to talk to her,' he thought.

Sita had not seen the monkey. Her thoughts were far away as she looked at the moon. 'How happy we were in our little hut in the forest! When will Rama come and rescue me? Will I still be alive?' she wondered, her heart filled with grief.

Since she had been brought to Ashokvan about four months ago, each day had been exactly like the previous one. Ravana came to plead with her or threaten her. 'Marry me. I will make you my queen. All the jewels I have stolen from the gods will be yours,' he said every day. After a while, he would lose patience and storm off.

But even then there was no relief. All day long, the demonesses changed their shapes to frighten her, cajole her and coax her in turn. Sita just sat as still as a rock. She spoke only to the trees in the Ashokvan, prayed and fasted, hoping Rama would come to rescue her soon. The demonesses guarding her would jeer and threaten, and she would console herself by thinking of Rama.

Today, however, had been different. Ravana had grown tired and given her a deadline. 'You have two months from today to make up your mind. If you refuse, I will cut you up into many pieces and the palace cooks will cook you for my dinner,' he had thundered. Sita had not even lifted her face to look at him. 'I will rather die than even think of marrying you,' she had whispered. Ravana had stamped off, cursing.

Sita had been troubled by his threat. But just now, she did not know why, there was a sudden sense of peace in her troubled heart.

Hanuman waited quietly till all the demonesses guarding Sita dozed off. Then he hopped on to a branch right above Sita and very softly, so as not to wake them, began chanting Rama's name. 'A noble prince named Rama, son of King Dashrath of Ayodhya, is the greatest hero to walk on earth. O Rama! O Rama!'

Sita could not believe her ears. Rama's name in this garden full of demons! At first she thought she was dreaming, but no, she could still hear the chant. She looked up and was surprised to see a tiny monkey with gleaming golden eyes, murmuring to himself.

'Who are you? How do you know about my lord, Rama?' asked Sita, with a worried frown. She wondered if this was Ravana's latest trick.

Hanuman folded his hands and spoke, 'I am Hanuman, a servant who serves your lord. I have been sent by Rama. He asked me to give you this ring.'

Sita cried out with joy as she recognized her husband's ring, and then clapped her hands on her mouth. She spoke in a whisper. 'Tell me, dear little monkey, how is my lord? Does he think of me? When will he come to rescue me?' In spite of herself, tears spilled out of her eyes.

Hanuman could not bear to see her cry. 'Do not cry, my gentle lady. Rama is going to rescue you very soon. I came to Lanka to make sure you were here. A huge army of monkeys and bears is waiting on the seashore. We will attack this city soon. I must go now, but we will be back in full strength.'

'Wait,' said Sita. She took a pin from her hair, which Rama had carved out of a branch during the happy days at Chitrakoot, and gave it to Hanuman. 'Give this to my lord. I have nothing else to give him, but give him this and tell him to come soon.'

Hanuman folded his hands together and took the pin. Then he bade her farewell, and quietly disappeared into the night.

Having fulfilled his mission, Hanuman felt enormously cheerful. 'Time to celebrate,' he thought, 'but how?' As he sat on the palace wall thinking, he had an idea and smiled mischievously. 'I will leave some mark of my visit before I go,' he said to himself, his eyes twinkling with glee.

He looked around. Beyond the walls of Ashokvan was another more elaborate garden of jewels, which lay right in front of Ravana's chamber and was brightly lit with many jewelled lamps. But while Ashokvan was filled with lovely trees, this was all man-made. He could see the dark shapes of some demons walking beneath the artificial trees.

Hanuman smiled to himself. He took a flying leap, landed on a golden tree nearby and began to break the silver branches off. He stamped his foot on the crystal pond and broke it, and then picked out the jewelled fish and began to crush them.

The demons came running up. If anyone spoiled this garden, Ravana's wrath would be fearful. 'Monkey! Catch the little monkey,' they yelled, as the palace guards came charging out.

But Hanuman was too quick for them, and he was having too much fun. As the guards came near him, he suddenly made himself so big that they ran away frightened. When they gathered more guards and came to find him, he made himself so tiny that he slipped out of their hands. He made them chase him all around the garden as he broke one jewelled lamp after another.

Hearing all the shouts and cries, Ravana came roaring out into the garden and was furious to see how it had been damaged. 'Bring this pest to me, or I will have all your heads,' he thundered and went back to his courtroom.

All the demons left their dinners and came out. Demon-generals as huge as giants, warrior demons who could fight the gods, and princes of the royal family—all came one after the other, but Hanuman swatted them like flies, despite his small size.

Finally, Hanuman decided that he had had enough of this game. It was time for something new. He let himself be caught when one of the demons used the Brahmastra against him. 'I have a boon from Brahma by which I can free myself any time, but I will pretend to be helpless. That way I will get to meet Ravana,' he thought happily.

The demons were overjoyed to have caught him. 'Finally, the little pest is in our grasp,' they shouted. They tied him firmly with a strong rope and dragged him to Ravana's court.

Hanuman tried to look helpless and frightened as he was pulled along, all the while looking around him with alert eyes.

The court was magnificent. Golden pillars glittered, and the floor was made of shining silver. Many powerful demons sat around. And then he was flung to the floor.

He looked up, and right in front of him, on a huge gleaming throne that glittered with many gems, sat Ravana, his ten faces scowling down at Hanuman. Battle scars covered his chest and his eyes were red with rage. 'You miserable little worm, why were you destroying my garden? Tell me just now or else I will tear open your chest and eat your heart.' His voice boomed around the hall and echoed all through the city of Lanka.

Hanuman thought quickly about what he should say. 'I am Hanuman, a servant of Rama,' he said proudly, holding his head high.

Ravana was so surprised that he was speechless. Hanuman continued calmly, 'You call yourself a great king, and you take pride in your fighting skills. Yet you are no better than a thief who steals another man's property. Let Sita go, or you will have to face your end very soon. Rama is the greatest warrior on earth and he will crush you like an ant under his foot. There is an army of monkeys and bears waiting on the shore and they will be here in a matter of days to destroy you and take Sita back.'

The demons were frozen with terror when they heard Hanuman. Never had anyone spoken to their king like this!

Ravana jumped up from his throne, caught hold of Hanuman's neck and shook him like a rat. 'I will kill you here and now,' he snarled.

His ministers came running up to him and fell at his feet. 'O king, do not kill the messenger. It is not fit for you, the greatest of all kings, to stoop so low.'

Slowly, Ravana let Hanuman go. 'Let him go,' he said, an evil glint in his eye. 'But set his tail on fire. That way we will not have killed him, but he will die all the same!'

The demons caught hold of Hanuman, still tied up, and dragged him out of the palace. They grabbed his tail, wrapped it in a cloth and dipped it in oil. Then they set it on fire. They made him walk through the streets of Lanka, prodding and jostling him with sticks to push him forward, and jeering and laughing at his plight.

'Let them laugh. I will soon show them what I can do. But first let me see this city properly,' thought Hanuman, letting out little whimpers and squeals so that the demons thought he was scared and in pain. He was a bit surprised that his tail did not hurt at all, and decided he should take advantage of that.

The reason why the fire did not harm Hanuman was because Sita had overheard the demons yell and scream as they set

Hanuman's tail on fire. She had asked Agni, the god of fire, to protect Hanuman so that the fire would not harm him.

As Hanuman walked on, he carefully took note of the layout of the fortress, how many demons were on guard, what weapons they carried, and other such details which would be useful later.

After a while, Hanuman decided he had gathered enough information and it was time to have some more fun. With a deafening roar, he jumped high into the air, giving the demons who were following him a fright. He took a deep breath, and his body grew to an enormous size so that ropes binding him snapped like threads. His burning tail was as long as a snake, and now he began to swing it around and everything he touched caught fire. Trees, houses, curtains of silk, chariots and stacks of grain—all went up in flames. He dragged his tail along a row of roofs, and soon they were all burning merrily.

The wind laughed with joy and came to help Hanuman. It blew the flames along, setting the golden mansions alight. The gold soon turned molten red, and the silver began to blacken with the smoke as the magnificent city of Lanka burned. Hanuman leapt from one mansion to another where the wind had not reached, leaving a trail of flames behind him.

'Burn, Lanka, burn, but let Ashokvan stay safe,' said Hanuman, heading back towards the sea. He plunged his tail into the cool waters to extinguish the fire. He looked back at the city, now burning gold against the darkness. Demons, black shapes against the fierce light, ran helter-skelter in panic, trying to put out the flames with pails of water. Hanuman smiled, and taking a big leap, set of again for the mainland to inform Rama that Sita had been found.

Preparing for War

Hanuman flew swiftly back over the sea. He did not go back to the unit of the army he had been travelling with, but returned directly to Kishkinda, where Rama, Lakshmana and Sugriva were waiting for news.

The monkey-squadrons had already started coming back, all heavy-hearted about their failure to find Sita. There was a clamour when Hanuman walked into the courtroom where they were all assembled. He was dirty, covered in soot and had a burnt tail. But by the gleam in his eyes, they knew that he was the bearer of good news. They offered him food and water, but Hanuman was anxious to tell them the news first.

'I saw Sita. She is well, but she is a prisoner in Ravana's palace, in Ashokvan, and guarded by many demonesses. She asked me to give you this, my lord,' he said, and gave Rama her hair ornament. 'She is very unhappy and frightened, and waits eagerly for you to rescue her.'

Rama looked at the wooden pin in his hand. His heart was full of sorrow, but he did not show his grief to the monkeys. 'We must prepare for war,' he said, in a low voice full of sadness and anger. 'Hanuman, did you get a chance to look around the city and its fortifications?'

Hanuman reported on all that he had seen. He told Rama and the monkey-generals of the size and might of Ravana's army, the structure of his fortress, the number of guards, the moats, the gates, and the huge catapults and drawbridges that spanned the rivers. 'The city is very well-guarded,' he said, 'but I created a little trouble!'

He narrated how he had destroyed Ravana's garden and then set the city on fire. All those present in the courtroom burst into laughter. But soon they stopped laughing and began to discuss the preparations for the war. 'Death to Ravana, the king of demons!' they shouted. 'Long live Rama!'

Preparations for war began. Thousands of monkeys were armed, trained and divided into squadrons. For days the only sound that could be heard in Kishkinda was the clang of metal on metal, as weapons were repaired and new recruits trained. The bear-squadrons assembled as well, and the scouts started marking out paths to the sea.

Finally, the great march began as thousands of monkeys and bears set out from Kishkinda under the flags of Sugriva and Rama, and began their long march to the south. The eagles flew ahead to keep watch on the path.

Meanwhile, in Lanka there was panic. 'How could a little monkey set our great city on fire and escape?' wondered all the demons, shaking their heads in worry.

Ravana ordered the entire city to be on alert for any enemy attacks. Hundreds of demons were sent to keep guard all along the sea coast so that no one could reach the island unseen. Others were set to work to repair the damaged buildings and fortifications.

Meanwhile, Ravana called a council of war. 'We must be prepared for war. That little monkey would not have had so much courage unless there was an army waiting to attack. Bring out all the new weapons from the armoury and distribute them to the army,' he ordered.

The prospect of war always thrilled the demons. Ravana's sons, brothers and uncles were overjoyed, but each had only one worry. Who would be chief of the war council? Since Ravana had become king, the demons had never lost a battle, and fame and fortune always went to the council chief. Each demon set out to flatter and praise Ravana so that he could gain that position of power.

As one demon after another stood up and praised Ravana's great bravery, poured scorn on Rama's foolhardiness and prophesied a great victory, there was only one face which looked worried and sad.

This was Ravana's younger brother Vibhishan. When his turn to speak came, he spoke plainly. 'I believe, O king and dear brother, you should think about this war with a clear mind. We are in the wrong. We are holding Sita captive. Return her to Rama or else we will face a terrible defeat. See how bad omens hover over our city…' Ravana's face turned black with rage, but Vibhishan carried on unconcerned. 'Listen to my advice, brother. You are a great king. Make peace with your enemy. Return Sita and apologize to Rama. This war will bring you no glory.'

'Out! Out of my sight, you weak miserable coward, you traitor!' Ravana yelled, dashing the goblet in his hand to the floor. 'Are you a demon or a human in disguise? I am ashamed to call you my brother. How dare you ask me to bow before a mere man, when even the gods fear my might! And what a man—a weakling who was driven out by his father; who relies on an army of monkeys and bears to fight me! Get out at once before I kill you!'

Ravana's sons and other brothers rose from their seats, drawing their swords as if ready to follow Ravana's command. Showing no signs of fear, Vibhishan bowed his head to his brother and quietly left the room.

Vibhishan left the royal city of Lanka at once and flew across the sea, taking with him four loyal and mighty demons, who were brave as well as kind. They reached the mainland and found their way to where Rama, Sugriva and the monkey-army had camped for the night as they marched to the coast.

Vibhishan walked into the tent where all the generals were assembled and introduced himself. 'We have come to you in all humility,' he said. 'We know Ravana has done wrong. Forgive us and allow us to serve you.' He explained why they had left, and then there was silence.

Vibhishan looked around. The expressions on the faces of his listeners were not very friendly. Lakshmana watched him with a frown. He was suspicious of these five demons. Sugriva, Angad, the monkey-general, and Jambavaan, the bear-general, also did not seem very keen to have the demons on their side and watched them with narrow, alert eyes. Vibhishan heard a whisper. 'They are a very cunning race.

We have yet to cross the sea. Maybe they have come to drown us or to pass on information about our numbers and weapons.'

Gazing around the room, Vibhishan saw the first friendly face as Hanuman nodded to him, a smile in his eyes. Then his eyes came back to the man in front of him.

Rama smiled and reached out his hand. 'You have come to me as a friend. Once a man surrenders himself one should trust and accept him. I have always believed in this. From today, you are as dear to me, Vibhishan, as the rest of my brothers.'

Crossing the Ocean

Finally, after many days of weary marching, Rama and the army reached the shore. They were all filled with great excitement when they saw the vast blue waters.

Rama asked all the members of the council and the generals to come down to the shore with him. As Sugriva, Lakshmana, Vibhishan and the generals gathered on the empty beach, the dolphins playing in the waters nearby were surprised at this sudden crowd of people on their shore and raised their heads out of the water to hear what was being said.

Rama and his friends stood on the edge of the water, looking out at the open sea. This was the crucial challenge—how would the vast army cross the sea?

For a while they stood in silence, looking at the tiny speck in the distance that was Lanka. Finally, Rama spoke. 'We will have to build a bridge which can carry our army. There is no other way across.'

'But how can we build on these turbulent waters?' asked Sugriva.

'The only way that we can achieve this is if the gods are willing to help us. Let us pray to the sea god for his blessings, for only then can we succeed,' replied Rama.

All of them sat down to pray. Rama, his eyes shut in prayer, spoke in humble tones, 'O lord of the seas, master of the waves, we beseech your kindness. Show yourself to us so that we, your humble worshippers, may be blessed. Stop your waves, so that we may be able to build a safe passage across your waters.'

Rama and the others fasted and prayed for three days, but there was no sign of the sea god. Instead, the waves became larger and more fierce and lashed at them.

Finally, Rama, his eyes glowing with anger, rose to his feet. 'If the lord of the seas thinks we are weak because we are praying to him, we should show him that we can be strong too when the need arises,' he declared.

He picked up his bow, drew an arrow, and running down to the water's edge, shot it out to sea. The arrow skimmed over the surface of the water at such great speed that the waves were set on fire. Soon the water was steaming, the sea began to churn and bubble, and great plumes of smoke rose from the surface. Finally, it became so hot that the sea god could bear it no more.

They heard his voice echoing from the depths. 'My lord, forgive me. I cannot stop my waves, just as the earth cannot stop moving, the air flowing and the light gleaming. Earth, air, ether, water and fire—these five elements must follow the laws of nature, for without these the world will die. I cannot stop my waves from rolling for more than a few seconds, but I will make a passage for your bridge. Let the monkeys bring boulders and trees down to the shore. I will help them.'

The army was called and ordered to collect boulders and rocks. They jumped up and ran to the forest. Bears lumbered up and down with huge tree trunks that they had uprooted. Some monkeys climbed a hill and began rolling down the rocks to the shore, shouting and squealing with glee. The smaller monkeys gathered pebbles to hold the large rocks together and fill in the gaps. Squirrels ran about with tiny pieces of wood in their mouths and the eagles showed them where to put them.

Meanwhile, another group of monkeys, supervised by Nal, Sugriva's chief engineer, pushed the boulders collected on the shore into the sea. As the monkeys threw the giant boulders into the sea, the water splashed sky-high and the noise of the waves was drowned by the monkeys' shouts of glee. Dolphins sent by the god of the sea swam near the construction site, making sure that the waves remained calm and the boulders were not washed away.

After the giant boulders had been set into the bed of the sea, the monkeys piled the smaller rocks and logs on to them in careful formation so that a solid base was build. The top of the bridge was filled in with small pebbles and grass to make a smooth surface.

Once the first part of the bridge was built, the monkeys rolled the giant boulders along that to build the next section. They worked all day and night for three days, and finally the long bridge over the sea was complete and shone like a silver ribbon across the blue expanse.

Sugriva called his army together, and led by Rama and Hanuman, the long columns set off to Lanka, cheering loudly as they marched.

Before the Battle

In Lanka, meanwhile, Ravana's guards, posted to keep watch on the shore, had reported how the bridge was being built and how the monkey-army was crossing it.

Bugles sounded the war cry as thousands of demons marched out of the city gates, armed and in neat order. 'We will crush these humans and their pathetic army of monkeys,' the generals roared, but the common soldiers were not so sure. 'If one little monkey had managed to create such havoc, what would an army do?' they wondered.

Gulls screeched and the sky was black with thunder as the two armies came up face to face. The demons, their faces crooked with rage, were greater in number and size. They rumbled and roared as they stood on the slope outside the city and looked down upon the monkey-army gathered on the shore.

The monkeys were calm and full of dignity. 'We will win this war because we are fighting for what is right and good, we are fighting for Rama,' the monkeys reminded themselves as they faced the giant demons. Though their army was smaller and the demons were larger in size than them, the monkeys felt no fear in their hearts. Their eyes shone with valour and zeal.

The drums of war began to roll on both sides. Flags waved under the stormy sky, but were soon soaked as the first drops of rain began to fall. Battle cries rose and mingled with the sound of thunder, and rang all through the island.

Raindrops fell thick and fast as the two armies eyed each other. While some of the monkeys marched straight ahead and faced the demons, the others ran across the white sand in different directions and soon surrounded the city from all sides.

Rama called Angad, the prince of the monkey clan, and asked him to take a message to Ravana. 'O Angad, tell Ravana that Rama awaits at his door, ready to battle. Tell him his end is approaching and he should prepare for it. He has troubled the world for too long with his wickedness. Tell him to come out and fight. But if he fears death, then tell him to return Sita to me and he can escape with his life.'

Angad flew into Ravana's palace where the demon-king was sitting on his agate throne, dressed in robes of red silk, waiting for news of the battle. There were very few demons in the courtroom with him, as most of them had gone out with the army.

When Angad flew in, they looked up in surprise. Angad stood in front of the throne and spoke clearly. 'Listen, O Ravana, wicked king. I have come as Rama's messenger. You have two choices. You can return Sita and ask for his forgiveness, or you can die in battle at the hands of Rama. If you choose the latter option, I would advise you to say farewell to your kinsfolk and to perform your funeral rites yourself because none of your race will be left to do them.'

Ravana flew into a rage 'Seize him... Kill him.' Two demons rushed at Angad, but he rose into the sky, carrying them both with him. In mid-air he swung them around until their necks were twisted and then flung them to the ground.

The demons left in the courtroom were filled with fear, but they tried to hide it. 'Another monkey who dares to speak to Ravana like this!' they thought, nervously biting their claws.

Rama heard what Angad had to say while he looked at the vast army of monkeys and bears spread out before him with calm eyes. Then he ordered them to begin the battle.

The First Battle

Shouting 'Victory to Rama! Victory to Sugriva!' the monkey-army rushed towards the golden city. They hurled giant boulders against the city gates, which soon broke.

Meanwhile, another section of the army attacked the demon-army, who carried spears the size of tree trunks. The demons jabbed the monkeys with their spears and tried to kill them with their swords, but the monkeys were too quick for them. They leapt high up in the air and then jumped down on the demons, biting and clawing them till they howled with pain and fled the battlefield. 'Kill the monkeys! Charge!' thundered the demon-generals who rode on elephants, but their soldiers continued to flee from the battlefield.

Bugles and trumpets blew and drums rolled as the two armies fought, and soon the field was covered with blood and dead bodies.

Rama, Lakshmana, Sugriva, Angad and Hanuman fought the demon-generals. Each encounter was so fierce that the gods came out to watch.

Rama sent an unending shower of arrows from his quiver, destroying hundreds of demons. No one could come near him. The demons tried to pour hot oil from the sky and shoot poison darts at him, but Rama's arrows formed a shield around him and not even a ray of light could break through the shield and touch him.

The hours went by and the sun set in a burning ball of fire. Though it was usual to stop fighting after sunset, the demons were desperate and fought on. They thought it would be harder for the monkeys to fight after dark in an unfamiliar place, and so they wanted to make the most of the opportunity.

The demons lit torches and flares, and came hurtling down the hills. In the surrounding forests, jackals howled as they sniffed blood in the air.

But what the demons had not realized was that the monkeys could see very clearly in the dark. They leapt upon the demons and tore them apart with their sharp claws and teeth. The demons, on the other hand, could not see in the dark. In the confusion, demons killed one another as spears flew around the battlefield.

When Ravana's son, Indrajit, realized that the demon-army was losing more soldiers than their opponents, he made himself invisible and rushed to the battlefield, though it was well past the hour when the battle should have ended for the day. However, he could not bear to see so many of his soldiers killed. He sent a stream of arrows at the monkeys, but they could not attack him as they could not see him and had no idea where the arrows were coming from. In the panic and confusion, they stopped attacking the demons, who leapt on them with renewed enthusiasm.

Rama and Lakshmana, realizing what was happening, sent their lethal arrows in a circle all around the battlefield so that they could hit their invisible opponent wherever he was. But Indrajit avoided all the arrows.

Then, as Rama and Lakshmana paused to discuss what to do, they felt two slimy snakes wrapping themselves around their throats. They tried to push them away, but the snakes held their necks so tightly that they began to lose consciousness and fell down in a tangle of limbs.

Indrajit laughed, a sudden sound coming from nowhere, and sent another serpent-arrow to bind their legs. The brothers lay on the ground, helpless and nearly unconscious as the monkeys watched fearfully. 'What has happened to them?' they asked each other.

Seeing that the monkeys were distracted, the demons began to scream with glee and rushed at them with clubs and spears. Some demons jumped up in the air and came crashing down on the smaller monkeys.

Suddenly, a huge gang of black monkeys appeared as if from nowhere. While the other monkeys looked at them in surprise, they started attacking the monkeys in Rama's army. These were demons who had changed their forms to take the monkeys by surprise. Faced with so many difficulties, the monkey-army began to lose their will to fight. Slowly, the demons began to overpower them.

'What is going on?' 'What shall we do?' the monkey-generals asked one another, fending off a shower of flying rocks. 'Rama and Lakshmana are lying helpless! All will be lost now,' one general cried above the noise of horses neighing and elephants trumpeting.

The demons charged forward, thrilled that they were regaining lost ground. They beat their drums, blew their huge conchs and rattled clubs and iron spikes. The monkeys began to waver and fall back. Some surrounded the two brothers and began to howl. Many ran around in different directions, not sure of what to do.

Indrajit, satisfied that victory was guaranteed, drove back to the city to give his father the good news. 'It is almost over, my lord,' he said, striding into the courtroom. 'Rama and Lakshmana are unconscious, victims of my serpent-arrows.

The magic is weaving its black web over them, and it is only a matter of time before they are dead.'

Ravana, thrilled, hugged Indrajit. 'You are a worthy son,' he roared. He turned to one of the demonesses in the court. 'Take Sita to the battlements and force her to look down at the battlefield. Let her see what my brave son has done to her silly husband. Then ask her if she is still unwilling to marry me!'

When Sita saw Rama and Lakshmana lying helplessly on the ground, for the first time she experienced a moment of doubt. All through her imprisonment, she had clung on to the belief that her husband would save her one day; that he would not let the evil Ravana go unpunished. But she knew that if she cried, the report would go back to Ravana. So she stood tall and strong, and said in a brave voice, 'No, they are not dead. My lord will rescue me yet and destroy Lanka.' Grumbling, the demonesses took her back to Ashokvan.

At the battlefield, Sugriva, Angad, Hanuman and Jambavaan worked hard to regroup their army again. Vibhishan tried to help them, but in their panic, the monkeys mistook him for another of Indrajit's demon forms and began attacking him until Hanuman came to his rescue.

Sugriva stood up in his chariot and addressed his army, 'Soldiers of Kishkinda, do not lose heart. Rama and Lakshmana are not dead, merely unconscious. They will not die, do not fear. We will win this battle and save Sita. Gather together once again and we will defeat these demons!'

Suddenly, there was a loud whirring sound, and the monkeys looked up to see a huge eagle flying down towards them. The monkeys tried to shield Rama and Lakshmana, thinking this was yet another demon. But the eagle called out to them, 'Fear not. I am Garuda. I have come to save Rama and Lakshmana.' Cheering, the monkeys cleared the way for him. As soon as Garuda's wings touched the brothers, the serpents vanished. Looking a bit dazed but otherwise recovered, Rama and Lakshmana stood up.

With a loud cry of triumph, the monkeys charged back into battle, led by Rama and Lakshmana. The demons were taken by surprise and soon the monkey-army gained the upper hand. The demons retreated, and the battle ended for the night.

When Ravana heard that the serpent-arrows sent by Indrajit had failed to work, he flew into a rage. 'Tell the demon-magician to make a model of Rama's head which looks so life-like that Sita will think it is flesh and blood. Send it to Sita on a platter. Once she sees Rama is dead, she will agree to marry me.'

The demons in his court nodded, but they were very worried about their king. 'Has he gone mad? We are losing hundreds of demons every hour yet he only thinks of marrying Sita!' they all thought, though none of them had the courage to say it. They glanced at one another, trying to persuade someone to get up and speak to Ravana.

Finally, one general, braver and more senior than the rest, got up to speak to Ravana. 'My lord, I have served you faithfully in this battle and in many others, so you know my loyalty to you and yours cannot be questioned. Please consider what I have to say.'

Ravana nodded grimly. 'Speak on,' he said.

'Send this Sita back to where she came from. She has brought so much chaos to our great land. No woman is worth that.'

Furious, Ravana jumped at his throat and began to shake him, shouting, 'Never, never, never… I will never send her back.' He shook the general so hard that he fell down, unconscious. Then Ravana calmed down. 'Wake my brother, Kumbhakaran,' he said. 'He will help us.'

Kumbhakaran

It was never an easy task to wake Kumbhakaran. This mighty giant slept for six months in a year, and it was practically impossible to wake him when he had not slept his full quota.

On Ravana's orders, hundreds of bugle players and drummers were sent into Kumbhakaran's room and told to play as loudly as possible. They did so, but only after positioning themselves carefully, so that they were not blown away by the demon's powerful breath. Then a hundred conches were blown near his ears, but this, too, had no effect.

Fifty demons were sent in to tickle Kumbhakaran's huge toes with palm leaves, but the sleeping demon just snored on peacefully. Next, Ravana ordered a hundred demons to poke Kumbhakaran in the belly with sticks. But Kumbhakaran gave such a huge snort that ninety-nine were blown away and the hundredth ran away in fright. Finally, when an elephant was brought in to walk on Kumbhakaran's body, the demon opened one eye and looked around wrathfully.

'Who dares wake me up?' roared Kumbhakaran, throwing the elephant off the bed. 'Tell me who is tired of life and wants to become mincemeat!' As he opened his mouth wide to yell, the attendants, who knew exactly what had to be done, began pouring barrels of wine down his throat, along with huge baskets of meat, fish and rice.

Once his hunger was satisfied, Kumbhakaran's temper cooled down and the ministers came in cautiously to speak to him. 'We woke you up, my lord, because Lanka is in grave danger, and your brother, the king, asked for you,' said the ministers, standing as far away as possible because they knew that Kumbhakaran usually belched mightily after his meal.

But the mighty demon was too shocked to belch. 'Our Lanka in danger? Which demon or god is so foolhardy that he will venture into our land?' he thundered.

'Not a demon, neither a god—it is a man who is causing all this trouble. His wife was brought here against her will by your brother, our king. And now Lanka is under siege, surrounded by monkeys and bears, led by this prince called Rama. Our troops are being defeated and killed. You must go into battle at once!'

Kumbhakaran leapt out of bed, squashing a few demons who were not quick enough to get out of his way. The elephant fled trumpeting loudly, as the demon strode into Ravana's courtroom.

'What is going on, brother? All was well when I went to sleep three months ago. I did hear you had imprisoned some woman who had insulted our sister, but I did not know that there was more to it. Now I hear that monkeys are laying siege to our city. How can monkeys, who run at the very thought of a demon, do this?' he asked Ravana.

'Yes, dear brother, you must save Lanka. It hurts our pride that we have not vanquished them already,' said Ravana, not meeting Kumbhakaran's glaring eyes.

'They say you have abducted a woman and her husband is waging war on us. Is that true?' asked Kumbhakaran loudly. The demons present in the hall looked away carefully. Ravana scowled, but did not reply.

'A great king like you stooping so low!' said Kumbhakaran scornfully, interpreting his brother's silence correctly. 'But you are my brother and my king. I will kill this enemy and save our race. But remember, brother, if I die in battle, it was a sin you committed when you stole another man's wife.'

Kumbhakaran picked up his spear, which was as tall as a tree, and marched at once on to the battlefield where the second day of fighting was under way. When they saw his massive and ferocious form lumbering up, the monkeys began to scatter in confusion. With a roar that shook the earth, the great demon jumped into the fray.

After the initial confusion, the monkeys and bears attacked Kumbhakaran systematically. The monkeys tried to climb on to him and stab him with their daggers, while the bears attacked his legs. But Kumbhakaran brushed them aside as if they were flies. Trampling dozens of monkeys under his mammoth feet, he charged towards Rama and Lakshmana.

'Watch out, here comes one of the greatest demon-warriors!' shouted Vibhishan, who knew what havoc his brother could wreak.

Rama turned and saw the huge demon. He began to shoot arrow after arrow towards Kumbhakaran. The arrows found their mark and cut off the demon's arms and legs. But even that was not enough to stop Kumbhakaran in his tracks. Instead he continued charging towards them, dragging himself on his stumps. Fountains of blood sprang from his mutilated limbs, but Kumbhakaran laughed loudly as he drew closer.

Rama took a deep breath, and thought for a moment. Ordinary arrows were useless against so powerful a demon; he would have to use the magic weapons Sage Vishwamitra had taught him to summon. He shut his eyes and said a prayer. Then he sent a single golden-tipped arrow straight at the demon's head. The arrow arched through the sky and sliced the huge head off, still roaring with laughter. The head shot up into the sky and then fell on the highest citadel in Lanka and burst into flames. Loud rejoicing broke out among the monkey-army, despite the fact that they had lost many scores of warriors in the brief encounter.

Indrajit

Through the window of his palace, Ravana saw his brother's head fly through the sky and burst into flames. 'Lanka, too, will burn soon,' he thought and was overcome by sorrow.

Indrajit saw his expression and knew his father was in despair. 'I will go,' he said. 'Do not despair, father, there are still many mighty warriors left in Lanka. I have defeated the king of gods, Indra; what are these little mortals compared to him? I almost killed Rama and Lakshmana with the serpent-arrows, it was only because Garuda intervened that they were saved. I promise that the next time I see you, I will have killed both of them and will come to you bearing their heads,' he declared.

Indrajit armed himself and bowed down for his father's blessings as he left the court. 'You are a worthy son! Be victorious!' said Ravana.

'Let the world watch and let the gods in heaven be witness as I put these two brothers to eternal sleep,' Indrajit said grimly and strode out of the court.

Indrajit's chariot rolled out to the battlefield, arrows flying from it like rays of light from the sun. Monkeys and bears were killed by the score. Their generals shot many arrows at him, but none of them could touch him. Rama and Lakshmana too shot at him, but to no avail. The whizz of arrows cutting through the air sounded like thousands of bees humming in unison.

Finally, Indrajit hurled the Brahmastra at Rama and Lakshmana. As it hit them, they fell down on the ground, unconscious. Before Indrajit could harm them further, Hanuman quickly whisked them away to a safe place.

The monkey-army was overcome by sorrow, and Indrajit triumphantly attacked more of them. Mercifully for them, the sky was darkening. The sun set soon, and Indrajit withdrew for the night.

Hanuman gazed in horror at Rama and Lakshmana, who slept as if they would never wake up again. 'How can we cure them?' he asked. 'Is there any cure?'

Jambavaan, the oldest general in the army, spoke slowly. 'Yes, there is one, the only cure for the Brahmastra. On one hill in the Himalayas, there grow four herbs, which together are known as the sanjivani. You need to go pick all of them— if you get only three, the cure will not work. Only these can make Rama and Lakshmana regain consciousness. But it is a long way to the Himalayas, and we need to get these herbs soon, for they cannot last too long in this state. Do you think you can do it?'

'Yes, I will,' said Hanuman firmly. 'Describe where the hill is and what the herbs look like, and I will get them to you by dawn tomorrow.'

Jambavaan did so in great detail, and Hanuman listened carefully. He left immediately and flew as fast as he could over the seas, and then over the huge landmass of India. Seeing how hard his son was trying to fly fast, his father, Vayu, sent favourable winds to speed him on his way.

It was the middle of the night by the time Hanuman reached the Himalayas. He found the hill of herbs that Jambavaan had described without too much difficulty, but in the darkness he could not see the plants the old bear had described.

'Are you hiding from me?' he asked the plants angrily. 'Are you Ravana's friends? Well, then, I will take the entire hill back with me. I do not want to waste time.' With one mighty pull, he lifted the hill up with one hand, and began the long flight south.

As he flew he could see the sky lighten, and he flew faster and faster. Finally, as dawn was breaking, he reached Sugriva's camp where many anxious monkeys had been awake all night, watching over Rama and Lakshmana. The soothing scent of the medicinal plants filled the air, and Rama and Lakshmana opened their eyes.

The monkey-army let out a roar of joy. Soon the bugles and drums sounded to mark the beginning of another day of battle, and the monkeys and bears went back to fight with renewed strength. But however bravely they fought, they were no match for Indrajit.

Apart from his great skill and courage, Indrajit also possessed many powerful weapons, which he had acquired through prayer and meditation. He could hide behind clouds, change his form and move with incredible speed. As the hours passed, he continued to kill hundreds of monkeys and bears.

In an attempt to save the soldiers and reduce their losses, his uncle Vibhishan attacked him. They fought a long duel; however, in the end, Vibhishan had to retire for he was gravely wounded.

Next, Indrajit turned towards Lakshmana. 'I will send you all to the city of Yama,' he said with a sneer. 'Salute the god of death because soon you will be his guest.'

Lakshmana was not intimidated in the least by his taunts. 'Fight like a true warrior instead of hiding in the clouds. Come face me and we will see who sends whom to the god of death,' he replied.

As he drew an arrow from his quiver, Lakshmana sent a silent prayer to Indra. 'If it is true that Rama is the bravest of all men, that he is the most truthful and noble, then may this arrow kill Indrajit,' he said. Then, raising his bow, he sent flying the Indrastra, a deadly arrow that never failed to find its target.

Flying through the air like a streak of lightning, the Indrastra cut Indrajit's head off. The monkey-army cheered loudly, and beat their drums and clashed their cymbals as the two armies withdrew for the night.

But Lakshmana felt sorrow for having slain a brave hero. 'Rest in peace, great warrior,' he thought in silent tribute.

Rama embraced his brother, wiping away the blood from his cheeks. 'You have performed a heroic deed. Now surely victory will be ours.'

Ravana

When Ravana heard late that night that his beloved son had died, he howled with grief and anger. 'Who is this Rama?' he yelled to the silent courtroom, where the demons still alive stood looking down at the ground. 'Is he a curse from my past life? I must kill him or die!'

His ten pairs of eyes glinting with cold fury, Ravana decided to go into battle. The king of demons kept vigil over his son's body all night. Then, as dawn was breaking, he put on his golden armour, which had been given to him by Brahma, picked up his mighty bow, and flew to the battlefield on his golden chariot drawn by black horses.

A clap of thunder echoed through the still air. The morning sun hid behind a dark ring and the sky darkened as Ravana's chariot entered the battlefield. The monkeys and bears gasped in awe when they saw the mighty demon-king, clad in gold and red, ferocious snarls of hate on his ten faces. His armour was dented with the scars of many battles. Following him were thousands of demons riding on horses, elephants and chariots. They were the last of the warriors left in Lanka.

As soon as he arrived on the battlefield, Ravana began his destruction of the monkey-army. They hurled boulders, rocks and spears at him, but nothing could even come near him. Ravana laughed when he saw them. 'Bravely done, little pests, but I do not want to waste time fighting beasts. It is Rama, your leader, who I will kill today.'

He drove his chariot towards where Rama stood. Hanuman and Lakshmana, who stood on either side of Rama, shot arrows at Ravana as he approached. These arrows hit several of his heads. Blood spurted out, but Ravana paid no heed and forced his way through the ranks. Finally, he stood face to face with Rama.

The earth fell silent, the wind stopped blowing, and the waves seemed to have ceased to roll, as all the gods came forth to witness this mighty battle between good and evil. They silently whispered their blessings to Rama. 'It was for this very moment that he was born on earth,' someone whispered.

They fought for hours as the monkeys, bears and demons watched, each side shouting for their king and leader. But later, even they fell silent and the only sounds that could be heard were the whirr of arrows as each warrior unleashed the whole range of magical weapons that they possessed.

Ravana let loose a stream of arrows towards Rama, who shot them to pieces with arrows from his bow. In turn, Rama sent arrows which sliced off some of Ravana's many heads, but they grew back at once.

Fiery arrows sped past, and their bows twanged, shaking the very earth they stood on. The arrows darkened the sky so that it became pitch-black though it was midday. Cutting through the dark, like bolts of lightning, were arrows that carried magical powers on their golden tips. Rama invoked a mantra and sent the Rudrastra, but it could not pierce Ravana's golden armour.

Ravana sent back the Asurastra on his arrows, which turned into wild beasts that roared and snarled and attacked Rama. But Rama retaliated with the Agneyastra, which burnt the beasts to cinders.

Ravana shot arrows which became serpents, but Rama killed them by sending a flight of eagle-arrows. Rama was fighting on foot, and he could not move as swiftly as Ravana did in his chariot. But despite this he matched Ravana bravely arrow for arrow.

At the height of the battle, a golden chariot suddenly appeared behind Rama, drawn by six green horses. The charioteer asked Rama to get in. 'The gods have sent you this chariot along with some weapons,' he said.

Black horses faced the green ones, and the battle became twice as fierce. The arrows flew at each other, clashed and fell on to the ground.

The hours passed. Though Ravana had fought with the gods and the greatest demons, he had never faced an opponent so unyielding. Rama seemed to be endlessly patient, always focussed and showed no signs of flagging, while Ravana's arms were getting weary and his breath came in ragged gasps.

Finally, with a prayer Rama sent the powerful Brahmastra flying towards Ravana. Screeching like an eagle, the flaming arrow pierced Ravana's golden armour and embedded itself right into his heart.

The oceans rose high in the air and overran the shore, mountains split open and began to pour out lava. The king of demons fell down on to the earth with a roar that shook all the three worlds.

Every creature on earth and in heaven trembled with fear at the uproar. Some wondered, had Ravana won? Did this mean the end of the world? Then, when they heard from the winds that Rama had put an end to the king of demons, they shouted with joy.

The sky cleared and the sun shone brightly like the first day of spring. The gods in heaven showered Rama with flowers. Those on earth could hear trumpets playing in heaven, rejoicing at the defeat and death of a man who had killed so many. The monkeys and bears went wild with joy, singing, dancing and clapping, kissing and hugging each other.

Sita, hearing the sounds of rejoicing as she sat in Ashokvan, knew that her husband had killed Ravana. She wept with joy and relief. Her long ordeal was finally over, and she looked forward longingly to meeting her husband again and living with him in peace and joy for the rest of their lives on earth. 'Nothing will ever part us now,' she vowed, tears of joy running down her cheeks.

Return to Ayodhya

From the battlefield itself, Vibhishan was brought directly to the palace and crowned king of Lanka. The monkey-army rejoiced. Some of Ravana's old ministers and the old general who had counselled peace came dressed in gold and jewels to bow before their new king. It would take time for peace and order to be restored in the city, but there was an air of hope. The demons of Lanka who had hidden in their houses during these days of war came out one by one to greet their new king.

Hanuman went to Ashokvan and brought Sita in a palanquin to Rama's camp. She was surprised that Rama had not come himself, but thought that perhaps he was too busy. Demons and monkeys jostled to catch a glimpse of Sita, of whose beauty there were innumerable tales. But when she came and stood before Rama, her eyes downcast with shyness, her heart full of love, he turned his face away.

Sita was stunned. She lifted her eyes and looked at Rama, unable to speak. Rama stood quietly for a while and then he spoke, his face stern and his voice cold, 'I have vanquished the enemy and rescued you. It was my duty and I have fulfilled it with the help of my brother and my brave friends. But do not think for a moment that I fought this battle just for your sake. I waged this war to fight the evil that had become a burden on this earth. Now that the war is over, you may live wherever you wish, but not with me. You have lived in another man's house for so long and I cannot take you back.'

Lakshmana stepped forward, protesting angrily, but Sita stopped him by raising her hand. Her eyes filled with tears, but she held them back. Lifting her head proudly, she said in a soft voice, 'My life, my heart, my breath are all yours and have always been only yours. Yet you, my lord, have broken my heart with these cruel words which are sharper than your arrows.'

There was a hushed silence. Rama spoke again, 'If you are as pure as you say, then you must test yourself in the sacred fire. If you are unharmed and if Agni himself tells me that you are pure, then I will take you back.'

Sita lifted her head proudly. 'Test me then. But I pray that after proclaiming me pure, Agni will consume me for I do not wish to live any longer if you doubt me. Light a fire, O Lakshmana, and let the flames take me.'

Lakshmana hesitated, waiting for Rama to stop Sita, but when he said nothing, Lakshmana ordered the soldiers to fetch some wood and lit a fire. Hanuman stood by, an anxious expression on his face.

Thousands of monkeys, bears and demons gasped as Sita stepped into the raging fire and sat down at its very centre.

'O god of fire, you know that I am pure, so take me within yourself,' she prayed.

The flames rose high till they were almost touching the skies. Sita could no longer be seen through the fiery curtain surrounding her.

Suddenly a white light flashed in the sky and Agni, the god of fire, appeared within the flames. 'My lord,' he said to Rama, 'she is as pure as fire, as water and as air. Take her and treasure her as your queen.'

As Agni vanished, Sita stepped out of the flames, wearing robes of spun gold. Golden ornaments sparkled on her arms and ears, and around her throat. She looked as beautiful as the morning sun. The monkeys and bears gave a loud cheer as Rama stepped forward and took her hand.

Rama smiled lovingly into her eyes. He spoke softly into her ear, 'I knew you were as pure as the sacred river Ganga. But so that no one could ever say anything about you and for the sake of the people of Ayodhya, I had to make you go through this trial by fire. You are my beloved wife and I know your heart belongs to me. But I had to do this to show the world how pure you are, and I hope you will understand and forgive me.'

A light rain fell from heaven as if to bless Rama and Sita. Many cheered, and the air was full of joy.

In the distance, drawing closer and closer was a chariot of flowers. It was a marvellous coach, soft and scented, and everyone gasped in wonder as it landed by Rama and Sita. The charioteer smiled at them and said, 'The gods have sent you this chariot to take you home to Ayodhya.'

Farewells were said, and many promises made by Sugriva, Hanuman and the others to come to Ayodhya, once they had met their families. Many in the gathering called out, 'Long live Rama and Sita,' as they stepped into the pushpak viman, which rose slowly into the sky and flew north over the ocean. The sky was golden-pink and the air was filled with music that floated down from heaven as the chariot drifted through the clouds.

As the chariot flew over the countries neighbouring Kosala, Rama, Lakshmana and Sita looked down at the familiar landmarks, which looked strangely different seen from the sky. 'There is the little hut where we lived so happily, and there is the river where we bathed... Look, the forest is full of flowers,' cried Sita. The deer came out of the forest and looked up at the golden chariot flying through the clouds. 'Be happy, Sita,' they said quietly.

As they passed over the Ganga, Sita gave thanks to the river for their safe homecoming, as she had promised when they crossed it to begin their sojourn in the forest.

After a while, the golden domes of Ayodhya appeared on the horizon, and suddenly they could all feel tears well up in their eyes. As the chariot neared Ayodhya, they could see people rejoicing in the streets. News of the great victory had travelled swiftly.

The people of Ayodhya were ecstatic with joy when they saw the chariot of flowers land. They rushed to greet Rama, Sita and Lakshmana. More than fourteen long years had passed since they had last laid eyes on the three of them, and they could not contain their joy.

Happiest of all was Bharata. Now finally he could give up his responsibilities to the true king.

The streets were covered with flowers. Lamps were lit in every house, along the balconies and at each window, which glowed and glimmered with happiness. Even to this day, we celebrate the day that Rama came home as Deepawali, the festival of lights.

Soon after, at a simple ceremony, Rama was crowned the king of Ayodhya.

Ayodhya prospered. The people in the kingdom were all healthy and happy. The rains came on time, and the harvests were larger than ever before. Trade flourished, and the country grew wealthy. The people shared it amongst themselves, so that none were too rich or too poor. As there was no space for greed or jealousy, everyone lived in peace. Rama was a just king, and the laws were fair. Everyone was busy and happy. There was almost no crime.

Even the weather conspired to make those years wonderful. The sun shone more brightly than ever, the skies were bluer, and the flowers bloomed in greater numbers than anyone could remember having seen before. There always seemed to be a fresh breeze blowing, the summers were mild, the winters warm, and the forests grew dense with new trees.

The people of Ayodhya were delighted with their young king, who was kind, just, brave and handsome. 'Heaven must be a kingdom like ours,' said the old men of the city as they sat under the peepal trees in the village squares.

Sita, too, was happy to be back in Ayodhya. She liked living in the palace with her mothers-in-law, and all her family and friends. She loved the beautiful palace, the gardens where peacocks danced and fountains played. But she often thought of the days she and Rama had spent in the forest. He was so busy with his royal duties that they spent very little time together, unlike the years where they had spent almost every hour of every day together.

'Remember, my lord, that lovely little hut in which we lived in Chitrakoot, that flower-bedecked roof in Panchavati?' she asked Rama one day, when he had finally come to her at the end of a long day. Rama, too, missed those blissful days in the forest with Sita and Lakshmana.

When he shut his eyes at moments like this, he could smell the sweet scent of the fresh forest air, hear the birds singing and the bees buzzing over wild flowers. But it was no use yearning for those simple happy days. Now he was king of Ayodhya and his duty was to look after his subjects. For hundreds of years his ancestors, each one a great king, had ruled over Ayodhya and he must follow in their footsteps. His own happiness was secondary. The people of Ayodhya must always be happy and content. He, their king, was like their father, and a father must look after his children, come what may.

And so the months rolled by happily.

The Second Banishment

Good times, however, cannot last forever, and soon there was trouble brewing.

One morning, when Rama entered the courtroom, he heard his ministers whispering amongst themselves. But when they saw him, they stopped abruptly and looked guilty.

Rama ignored this. His ministers knew he was a fair king who listened to them, and that they could come and talk to him if ever there was a problem.

However, soon Rama realized that the problem might be more complex than he had suspected. People lurked in the corners of the palace and spoke in quiet voices. At the monthly assembly, where the common people could come and tell him their problems and concerns, there were awkward silences. It was as if people had something to say but did not know how best to say it.

Later that evening, Rama summoned one of his ministers, Bhadra, whom he trusted greatly. 'What is the trouble? You must know that I realize that there is something wrong, but no one will speak to me about it.'

Bhadra remained silent.

'Speak,' said Rama. 'Do not be afraid. It is your duty to inform me of what is happening in my kingdom. You are my eyes and ears.'

'My lord,' Bhadra said hesitantly, 'the people of Ayodhya are full of praise for you. They say that by killing Ravana you have done a great deed, and that under your rule, life is wonderful again.' He fell silent after that.

'But there is something more, isn't there?' said Rama. 'Tell me the truth. You know I value truth above all else, even when it is sometimes hard to say or hear.'

Bhadra bowed his head. 'They say, my lord, that you should not have taken Queen Sita back. She lived in this demon-king's house for so many months. She should not be your queen.'

Rama was shocked to hear this. Sita had already been through the fire to prove her innocence, but that was not enough for the people of Ayodhya.

Bhadra continued. 'They say, how can we respect a king who has such a queen? If our wives had lived in a demon's home, we would not have taken them back. How can there be law in the country if we cannot respect our king?'

After Bhadra left, Rama called some other ministers he trusted. They, too, agreed with what Bhadra had said. One of them, an old man who had been Dashrath's minister too, told him, 'My lord, you must banish the queen. The people will have no faith in you as long as she lives with you.'

Rama stayed awake all night, his heart heavy with grief. Life is difficult when you wear the crown and sit on a throne. A good king has to think only of his people and rule in obedience to their wishes, especially where his own happiness is involved. He could disobey their wishes when he felt that it was better for them, but he had to listen to them where his own behaviour was in question, even if it meant sacrificing his own desires.

The night passed slowly. 'I want to go back to Chitrakoot again,' thought Rama longingly. 'How simple and happy life was there!' But he knew that that was impossible. Being a king was not something one could give up on a whim. Now his responsibility was to ensure his subjects were happy, even if it meant misery and grief for him.

Finally, as dawn was breaking, Rama reached a decision.

He rose early, and called Lakshmana to him. Without looking at his face, he said, 'Take Sita to the forest. Leave her at Sage Valmiki's ashram.' He could sense Lakshmana start in horror, and raising his hand to prevent him from protesting, he said, 'Please do not ask me to explain. I have thought about it and this is what has to be done. Just do what I ask. As your king and elder brother, I ask you to do this. If you disobey me in this difficult task, I will know that you do not love me.' As Lakshmana left the room horrified, Rama cried as if his heart would break.

Lakshmana did not know what to do. After many hours of worried thought, he finally decided that he had to do what his brother had asked. His faith in his brother was so great that he knew that Rama could never do something evil. There must be a sound reason behind this decision. But he did not have the courage to reveal to Sita what he was about to do. Instead, he suggested that they go for a long ride in the forest.

Rama stood at his window and watched the chariot as it disappeared down the streets of Ayodhya. His heart was heavy with sorrow, yet he had to continue attending to his duties. What else could he do? He had bowed to the wishes of the people of Ayodhya, even though it caused him so much pain. A king had to do what his people asked. Otherwise, he did not deserve to rule. His beloved wife was going to live alone in the ashram. He knew that Sage Valmiki would look after her as if she were his own daughter, but Sita would be heartbroken without him. It seemed that despite their great love for one another, the two of them were destined never to live together in peace. 'O Sita, will I ever see you again?' he thought. The same forest which had given them so much happiness was now taking Sita away from him, and he—such a mighty king—could do nothing but cry quietly, hiding his tears so that no one could see his sorrow.

Sita looked around her happily as the chariot left the fields of Ayodhya. The forest gleamed ahead like a vast sea of trees.

The last time she had seen it was when they were flying over it in the chariot of flowers. The trees had looked so tiny then. Now, as the chariot entered the heart of the forest, she could see the leaves and the flowers she loved so well, the vines that hung like ropes from the branches. The birds called loudly as they flew around the treetops and a herd of deer watched their chariot race by.

Sita wished Rama was with her, but she understood that he was very busy now. It was sweet of Lakshmana to take her out. After the fourteen years they had spent together, they were as close as brother and sister could be. And to him, she could speak of her most private thoughts. She talked to him about Rama as their chariot sped through the forest, about how proud she was of the way he conducted himself as king.

Lakshmana looked straight ahead at the path. He could not bear to talk to Sita. He was afraid even to meet her eyes lest he broke down. 'How happy she looks. She does not know as yet that she is going away to live in the ashram forever,' he thought.

Sita wanted to halt and gather some flowers that were growing in the meadows along their path but Lakshmana refused. He wanted to get this journey over as soon as possible. When Sita, taken aback at his rough tone, looked at him, she saw that he was crying.

'What is the matter, my dear brother?' she asked gently, suddenly aware that something was terribly wrong. 'Tell me what is wrong. I am sure my lord Rama can put it right.'

'No, he cannot,' said Lakshmana shortly. 'He cannot, for he has caused it.'

'Do not say so, my brother. What has he done?'

'O, I wish I had died before seeing such a day... But he is my king, and I have to obey him. O gentle sister, forgive me for what I am going to do now for I cannot forgive myself.' He paused and then spoke with great difficulty. 'I have been told to leave you at Sage Valmiki's ashram. You must live there from now on.'

Sita did not say anything at all. She kept watching the trees and flowers for a while. Then she spoke in a voice that was so soft that Lakshmana could hardly hear her. 'If that is my lord's wish, I will happily live at the ashram. He must have a good reason to ask me to do so.'

Lakshmana was amazed by her strength. She did not cry, and though her eyes were sad, her lips did not quiver.

At the ashram, Sage Valmiki was waiting for them. As they dismounted, he stepped forward to bless Sita. 'I saw in my mind's eye that you would come today. Do not be sad, my child. This ashram will bring you peace. We will look after you as well as we can.' He looked at Lakshmana and there was pity in his eyes. 'You can leave now.'

Lakshmana got into the chariot without meeting Sita's eyes. He did not look back until the chariot was some distance away, just where the ashram disappeared from view on the winding forest road. As he looked back, Sita seemed so small and helpless under the tall trees as Valmiki led her into the ashram.

At Valmiki's Ashram

The days passed slowly for Sita as she began to learn the ways of the ashram. Though she had lived in the forest for fourteen years, this time it was entirely different. Earlier, Rama and especially Lakshmana had taken care of her and protected her. Now she was just one of many women in the ashram. Valmiki treated her lovingly, like his daughter, but not as a queen. No one else in the ashram knew who she was, and though they all were affectionate and friendly, no one treated her any differently from the other residents.

There were many new things that Sita had to learn. A queen is not taught how to milk cows, or clean cowsheds.

But Sita did her best. She tried to keep busy, for whenever she had free time, her thoughts turned to her earlier stay in the forest. 'How happy I was with Rama by my side and Lakshmana to take care of us,' she would think and her eyes would brim with tears.

There was another change this time. Soon after she came to the ashram, Sita realized that she was expecting her first child. She did not know what to do, but the other woman at the ashram helped her when she felt ill. She longed to let Rama know that their child was soon to be born, but she had no way of informing him. 'Maybe he will send for me soon, or maybe he will send someone to find out how I am,' she thought, but no one ever came from Ayodhya.

The months passed, and one full-moon night, Sita gave birth to two handsome sons. She named them Lav and Kush.

They filled Sita's days with joy and laughter, and she busied herself taking care of them, singing to them and telling them stories. She still missed Rama, but it was a different kind of pain. Now that she had two babies to take care of, her days were full and happy.

The months turned into years without Sita realizing it. Everyone in the ashram loved the boys, and they never missed having a father around. The younger sages played with them, the older sages told them stories, and the women spoilt them. The boys kept everyone laughing with their pranks.

They grew up completely at home in the forest. From a very young age the deer and birds were their playmates. Lav would wrestle with baby tigers and Kush would race with the deer. They knew every part of the forest so well that they could find their way around the dense woods quite easily, even in the dark. At first, Sita would grow anxious when they went missing after sunset, but soon she learnt that they were able to take care of themselves. The two brothers would play with the deer and elephants, race around the trees, and swim across the stream to gather flowers for their mother. They would fish in the stream and climb the tallest trees to fetch their mother's favourite fruits.

The boys grew up fast, just like their father, and soon Sage Valmiki began teaching them how to use a bow and arrow. With amazing speed, they became great archers. All those who saw their progress marvelled. They became the official protectors of the ashram. They were so skilled that no demon or wild beast ever dared to stray near the ashram.

Valmiki taught the boys all he knew about warfare, not just about the use of weapons, but also how to think cleverly during battle. Soon they became warriors of great skill, just like their father, Rama, and their uncle, Lakshmana. After their warfare lessons were completed, Valmiki taught them the ancient scriptures and how to perform their religious duties. Sage Valmiki told them many stories so that they could learn from the tales of great gods and kings and legendary heroes. But the story that the boys loved best was that of King Rama and his queen, and how Rama had defeated Ravana to save her. The two brothers often sang the legend of Rama because they loved the story, but they did not know that Rama was their father and his queen was their mother.

And so the years went by peacefully. The boys had brought a new joy to the ashram and a rare laughter to the quiet walls. Like all other children, they played endless tricks on the people around them, especially as they looked so much alike that no one could tell them apart. And so they grew up, amidst nature, surrounded by the loving ashram-dwellers, and with no idea that they were sons of a great king.

The Aswamedha Horse

One day, after finishing their lessons, Lav and Kush were playing in the forest when they saw a white horse charging towards them.

Lav was always the more adventurous and he was the first to speak. 'Look, brother. What a beautiful horse! Let's catch it. We will take it to the ashram and keep it as a pet.'

They ran after the horse and finally managed to catch it. For a while they admired its white coat, flowing mane and taut muscles. Then, because it was growing dark, they decided to return to the ashram. They walked towards it with the horse, talking happily about what they would do with it.

Suddenly, Lav noticed something glinting in the animal's long mane. 'Look, Kush,' he said excitedly, 'it has a gold ornament around its neck. How strange!'

Kush looked closely at the ornament and exclaimed, 'King Rama's name is written on it.'

The boys looked at each other in surprise. 'What do you think it means?' asked Lav.

Suddenly the boys heard a loud clatter of hooves. Before they knew it, they were surrounded by warriors clad in silver armour. Though Lav and Kush did not know it, they were a team of skilled soldiers, specially selected to protect the horse.

Their leader rode up and surveyed the boys. He had a big moustache and bulging eyes. 'Let the horse go, boys,' he commanded. 'Can't you see it is a special horse? It has been sent out by King Rama for an ashwamedha yagna. Wherever the horse goes, the land becomes our king's. Anyone who tries to stop the horse has to fight us. So let go, lads.'

'Why? We have the horse. If you want it, you will have to fight us. Are you afraid of us?' said Lav with a naughty smile. Kush groaned, but prepared himself to back his brother up.

The soldiers began to laugh. One of them, a tall man with a crooked nose, said, 'Off you go, cheeky boy, or I will send you up that treetop with one slap.' He turned to point to a particularly tall one, and before he knew it he found himself whizzing towards it, propelled by a blow from the quiet Kush.

Now Lav and Kush began to laugh, while the soldiers looked amazed at their comrade hanging from a branch.

Once the soldiers had got over their shock, they charged at the boys. But the two brothers sent such a swift shower of arrows that several of them were wounded within moments. The rest ran, as if for their lives, back to Shatrughna, who was leading a squadron behind the horse's escort.

'Two young boys defeated your team? How can this happen?' he asked in disbelief. He consulted his generals, and they decided to go back to Ayodhya and return with a larger force.

Shatrughna went straight to the court to report to Rama. 'My lord, such a strange occurrence! Two young lads defeated our soldiers. I have come back to fetch more men. We cannot take the chance of being defeated again.'

There was much amazement in court. The courtiers whispered to one another. 'Amazing!' said Lakshmana. He turned to Rama, 'My lord, I want your permission to go see what is happening.' Rama willingly gave his consent, and Lakshmana left with the army the following day.

Back at the Ashram

When Lav and Kush returned to the ashram and narrated their adventures to Sage Valmiki, he was deeply amused, though he did not reveal this to the boys. He realized that fate was bringing Rama's sons to his notice. He counselled the boys not to tell their mother about the day's adventures. 'From what I know of King Rama, he will send his soldiers once again, but this time it will be larger force,' he said. 'You should be prepared for battle.' He was not worried, for he knew well that his two pupils were a match for any army.

Lav and Kush were very excited. It was like a game to them. Never had they thought that their quiet lives would change so suddenly and dramatically.

So when the army marched towards the ashram early the next morning, Lav and Kush were prepared. The other ashram-dwellers were, however, very frightened. 'Why is Rama attacking us? We have always lived at peace with him,' many of them cried out in terror. But soon their terror turned to glee as they realized that the two boys were more than able to defend themselves.

Lav and Kush fought like tiger cubs, and they routed the army within hours. The soldiers could not believe that the arrows that ripped through their ranks came from these two small boys. Many ran away from the battlefield, quite sure that the god of war was playing tricks on them.

When Lakshmana's chariot arrived at the centre of the battlefield, he was surprised to see two young boys terrorizing the army. Lakshmana suddenly recalled his own youth when he and Rama had to go to the Dandaka forest to fight the demons. He felt sorry for these brave boys and for their parents, because he knew he would have to kill them before they could do more damage to the army.

Lav and Kush saw Lakshmana lift his bow and fix an arrow. They looked at each other and smiled. 'Come, brave Lakshmana. We know who you are. Come and fight,' they said, laughing. Kush sent an arrow which knocked Lakshmana's helmet off.

Enraged, Lakshmana forgot his moment of compassion and sent a stream of arrows towards the boys. 'That will teach them to laugh at me,' he snarled.

But the two boys went down on their knees, and cut down each arrow he had sent towards them with theirs.

Impressed despite himself, but still furious, Lakshmana sent a fire arrow, but Lav quenched it with a rain arrow. Meanwhile, Kush had seen the monkey-prince, Angad, aiming at him, and he pinned him down with a shower of arrows.

Kush hurled a magic weapon. As soon as it hit the ground, it created hundreds of Lakshmanas, each commanding the soldiers to do something different. Confused, many of the soldiers dropped their arms and retreated, and others ran around the battlefield, crying out in fear. Each time they tried to attack the boys, a Lakshmana would come forward and stand in their way so that they had to lay their weapons down.

At the height of the confusion, Kush nodded at his brother. They came together and they sent forth a mighty lightning arrow. It rose in a great arc over the battlefield and struck Lakshmana right on his chest. With a cry of pain, he fell down on the ground, unconscious.

That was the end for the army. The soldiers who were still alive fled the battlefield and ran back to Ayodhya.

Rama listened to their report calmly, though he was deeply shocked. 'I will have to go now,' he declared.

'No, my king, you cannot leave the kingdom unprotected,' pleaded Bharata. 'Let me go. Should I fail, only then must you go. I, too, wish to serve you.' Rama thought for a while, and then agreed. 'You may go if you wish, but take Hanuman with you. These two young lads seem to be quite formidable.'

Lav and Kush, exultant after defeating Lakshmana, awaited the next attack. When they saw Bharata, they shouted for joy, and together they sent a magical arrow towards him. But Hanuman stepped forward to protect Bharata and diverted the arrow.

Kush was irritated by this giant monkey and raced towards him. He caught hold of him by his tail, swung him around until he was dizzy, and then tied him to a tree with magical ropes.

Hanuman was stunned by this treatment. He was one of the greatest warriors in the world, but these two boys seemed like warriors from heaven. 'These are not ordinary boys,' he thought, his head swimming. 'There is something special about them.' He knew there was also something strangely familiar about them, but he was too dazed to decide what it was, and he struggled to untie the ropes Kush had used to bind him.

Meanwhile, Lav had shot an arrow straight at Bharata that knocked him unconscious and off his chariot. 'That was easy,' he said happily to Kush.

'Now let us take this huge monkey to the ashram. Mother will be pleased with us and the ashram-dwellers will be happy to keep him as a pet,' suggested Kush.

The boys dragged Hanuman to the ashram by his tail, and the great warrior, who had slain so many ferocious demons, went with them meekly.

Unknown to them, the soldiers with Bharata had returned to Ayodhya and were reporting their defeat to Rama. Even as the boys walked slowly towards the ashram, tired after their battle, Rama was setting out of Ayodhya in his swiftest chariot, escorted by soldiers in fifty other chariots.

Rama and His Sons

Sita had been busy all day with the chores in the ashram and had not known anything of the great battle taking place. Wrapped in her own thoughts and her prayers, even the sounds of battle had not registered. Now, in the early evening, she was watering the plants when she saw her sons walking towards her, dragging something large behind them.

'Those boys!' she thought affectionately. 'What have they brought home now? Must be another bear cub. They love animals so much...'

'Look, mother! See what we have brought for you,' shouted the boys.

Sita looked more closely and she recognized the face she had first seen long ago in Ashokvan. She cried out, 'What have you done! Let him go! Untie him at once!' The two boys watched in amazement as their mother patted the head of their captive. 'O Hanuman, I hope my sons have not hurt you.' She turned to them in fury. 'If you have hurt my old friend...' she said, with a rare display of anger.

The two boys were too amazed to obey her. They had never seen their mother angry. And how did she know this monkey, who was now crying tears of joy?

In the stunned silence that followed, they heard clearly the sound of horses' hooves. There were swift commands. Rama had arrived, and now soldiers with gleaming swords and spears surrounded the ashram. The other residents of the ashram were weeping in terror, and even Valmiki had interrupted his evening prayers to see what the outcome of this strange day would be.

As Rama strode into the ashram, he was too angry to notice anything but that there were two boys holding ropes with which his old friend Hanuman was bound.

'Boys, let go of Hanuman,' he said in a voice which was very quiet but which still struck fear into every heart. 'And return my horse. You are boys; you should not play men's games. You have done great damage to my army and I will have to punish you for this.'

As he spoke, his anger melted away somewhat and he noticed where he was. Why, this was Valmiki's ashram. And standing before him, still as radiantly beautiful as when he had first seen her, was Sita!

The forest suddenly swirled around him and he felt he would fall down. His soldiers, having seen the magic weapons the boys had used, thought he had been attacked too, and came forward protectively. But he held out a hand to stop them.

'Sita, Sita,' he whispered, going forward.

The boys were surprised that Rama knew their mother's name. Apart from Valmiki, the other people in the ashram also looked on in amazement.

Sita came forward and drew her two sons along with her. 'These are your sons, Lav and Kush, my lord. Forgive them if they have done any harm.'

Rama could not speak. These two brave warriors who had defeated his entire army on their own were his two sons! Lav and Kush looked at each other in surprise. Rama was their father. This great king, of whom they had grown up hearing stories, whose fabled army they had taken on in battle and miraculously defeated—was their own father! But then why were they living in an ashram? Why was their mother not living with him?

Rama, his eyes full of tears, reached out his arms to embrace them. 'My brave sons! You are great warriors. I am glad to have found you, though you have grievously wounded my dear brothers.'

Sage Valmiki came forward. 'I will revive your brothers and all the slain soldiers,' he said. 'These two sons of yours are worthy heirs of your greatness. Accept them. Accept, too, your wife, Sita, who is as pure as Mother Earth herself. Take them back to Ayodhya with you, and rule in peace.'

Rama stood still looking at Sita. He knew she was the most noble and kind woman on earth, and he loved her more than anything else. But there were still his people to consider. What would they say if he brought her back to Ayodhya? His duty as a king was more important than his own desire as a husband.

Sita looked at Rama and saw the hesitation in his eyes. He still did not want to take her back! But he wanted his sons, and she knew that her sons would never leave her. The three of them looked so right together. They lit up the forest, shining in their heroic valour. It was she who did not belong in this happy picture.

Sita folded her hands and bowed her head. 'Mother Earth, if I have done any good in my life, if my heart is pure and my love for Rama true, then take me into you,' she said quietly.

There was a loud clap of thunder and the earth slowly split apart at Sita's feet. The cleft grew into a deep hollow, and slowly from it rose a golden throne which was held up by giant serpents. On the throne sat the goddess of the earth. 'Come, my child,' she said, and took Sita beside her on her throne.

The throne sank swiftly into the earth and the ground closed over them as if it had never opened up.

Lav and Kush watched in horror. They began to cry, overcome with grief that their mother, the only family they had known all these years, was gone so suddenly. Rama, too, shielded his eyes, which were full of tears.

'Do not feel sad for Sita. She belonged to the earth and now she has gone back to her mother. She will live happily forever since she is blessed by the gods. Her devotion to you is true and everlasting, Rama. She will meet you again in another life,' said Sage Valmiki.

Rama gazed at the place where Sita had disappeared for a long time and then he put his arms around Lav and Kush. 'Your mother was a great soul. Come with me, my sons.'

The boys turned to their guru. Sage Valmiki nodded. 'Go with your father, Lav and Kush. Your true place is with him. I have taught you everything I could in the ashram. Now it is time that you learn to be princes.'

Slowly and sadly, the boys bid goodbye to everyone at the ashram.

'Will someone please untie me,' said Hanuman suddenly, and the boys ran to him.

'Sorry we had to do this to you, great Hanuman,' they said.

The chariot raced through the forest, as the deer, the elephants and the tigers watched. 'Goodbye, brave Lav and Kush. Be happy in the palace but do not forget us,' they said, twitching their ears and swishing their tails, as the chariot headed towards the golden domes of distant Ayodhya.

Lav and Kush grew up to be brave warriors and gentle, kind men. Rama ruled for a thousand years. Before he died, he left his throne to Lav and Kush, who ruled well and wisely for many, many years.

Afterword

The great epic Ramayana is one of the oldest stories in the world. It is believed that it was first written down by the Sanskrit poet Valmiki about 2,500 years ago, though the story had been sung by bards and wandering storytellers for centuries before that.

In the preface to his version, Valmiki explains how he came to write the Ramayana. One day when Sage Narada came to his ashram, Valmiki asked him, 'O all-knowing Narada, tell me, who amongst the heroes of this world is the highest in virtue and wisdom?' Sage Narada replied, 'Rama is the one.' And then Narada told Valmiki the story of Rama, which he wrote down.

Later, the story of Rama, Sita and Hanuman was retold by many others, including Tulsidas in Hindi and Kamban in Tamil. The story is not confined to India but is well known in Sri Lanka, Indonesia, Thailand and all over South-east Asia. It appears in books, music, dance, plays, paintings, in hundreds of languages, and in thousands of versions.

Perhaps the reason for the Ramayana's great popularity is that it contains so many wonderful stories. The numerous exciting characters and their different tales are the reason that everyone likes to go back to the Ramayana time and time again. Children never tire of hearing about Rama's battles with the demons, cutting off Soorpanakha's nose, Hanuman crossing the ocean, and Kumbhakaran snoring in his giant bed over and over again. It is certainly one of my all-time favourites.

Today, the Ramayana is still popular in the form in which it first began: sung by musicians to a live audience. This is the form in which I love it most. I remember going to see Ramlila in our neighbourhood when I was a young girl. Everyone in the audience knew the story very well yet they listened with

rapt attention, as if the words were totally new. The actors—
our local postman, constable and grocer—were not very good
and kept forgetting their lines due to stage fright, but the
people in the audience would speak the dialogue for them.
When Ravana was about to carry Sita off in his flying chariot,
I could not help myself and called out, 'Sita, don't go with
him!' No one laughed at me because everyone was shouting
out the same warning.

I hope this version of the Ramayana will make you love
the epic as much as I do, and make you want to read other
versions of it as you grow older.

BULBUL SHARMA